The Totally Awesome Mega Writers Club
present

The Third
Compendium

Dear Jane

Happy Healthy 2022
Wishes
to you dear friend.

Thought you may like
to read the creative writers

book club

Love

from Kewstoke
Group.

Linda xxx

1

Cover photography by Carol Jadzia

©October 2021

Table of Contents

A note from the Editor

Books often have themes, throughout this book you may notice a running theme that is mainly to do with our furry and feathered friends. You see, we like animals in all of their forms, from cute little ducklings, right up to strange chimeric demonic beasts.

Some of the stories in this collection will give you a sparkle, they may even uplift your soul and give you a wistful desire to spread your wings and head into the sky like a baby bird that has just mastered the art of flight. Some however, will bind your ankles with rusted steel chains and drag you to the coldest depths.

Giving an author a theme can be a dangerous thing to do, even the most seemingly innocent idea can be twisted into something dark or evil or perverse, when given to an author who is not afraid to explore all aspects that make up our humanity. The results of this idea mashing can be read here.

So brace yourself, grab yourself a nice cup of tea, or maybe a lovely crunchy biscuit and then delve into the sweet, innocent, bizarre, dark and twisted minds of our authors. I promise you that although the stories contained herein may be a mixture of the light and the dark, our authors are actually the biggest bunch of smiling, laughing, hugging creatives you will ever meet! Bless the cheeky little lot of them!

GH

The First Hunt

By Margaret Ingram

I fall. The air grows fast and strong against my body. I stretch my wings naturally, without thinking and the wind finds me and slows me, makes me buoyant. I glide horizontally along the airways and turn as my wings shift and my feathers flex, my tail spreads and I slip sideways first towards the sun and then away. I move into another column of air which is rising above the trees and I glide upwards and circle round with just a small flex of my wings and tail. What, I wonder, will happen if I flex more on one wing than the other? Experimentation shows me the pattern of movement and I control my circle to stay within the rising column. I have no weight, my body is balanced by the air I fly within. High and higher I circle. My father circles near and calls and I answer his query. I don't want to go back to the ledge, I have no weight, I can do this forever. He calls again and I feel his power so I follow him out of the column and glide down to the shaded ledge which has been my home since forever. He lands ahead of me and I see him back-wing. When I am over the edge of the rocks I know so well I also feather my wings and drop onto the stones. I walk forward one step, two then fold my wings and stand. I have weight now and I can feel the tiredness in my shoulders, across my chest. He was right to call me in. I walk to the water in the hollow rock and drink, one scoop and, head back, down my throat, a second scoop, and a third. Enough.

Settling down by my mother in the nest, on the soft lining of fur from rabbits she and father ate before I was hatched, I settle and sleep. Mother and father have taken turns in watching over me since I hatched but now they both leave me. They are hungry and will hunt together for the first time in months. I will be hungry when I wake. Surely they will bring me food today, even though I can, at last, fly. My eyes close, my mind drifts off into the wind and I sleep as I dream of flying again.

They return as the sun is westering and the sky is golden and darkening. The ledge is shadowed and I am cool in the wind. They have eaten but bring me food saved from their prey. I tear at the still warm meat and gulp down rabbit and something else I cannot name. my empty belly is satisfied and I drink again then settle back to sleep. The older birds settle as well and one shields me from some of the wind. The temperature will drop soon, as the wasteland loses its heat to the night sky.

I am awakened by my father's calls in the dark of the night. The wind is strong and I wake and preen. My feathers are stronger, thicker each feed and I walk steadily towards the lip of stone as I see the world outside my old home in the starlight. I have not slept long and the land is still giving up its heat, making the wind swirl in columns and some dust dance in the rising air until it reaches the edge of the spiral and drops back, moving the sand slowly across the landscape.

The big birds are all launching onto the wind and I see several other young like me joining them. My parents launch and I follow, almost wing tip to wing tip with them. They ride the current down the rock face and out towards the sea. The wind is strong and gives me speed and ease. The other families are spreading out and we angle to my right slightly. I watch the land below and see it turn from rocky waste with few trees into undulating dunes with some grasses and then we are over the edge of the sea and the air is rising, carrying us up and on. We use our wings occasionally to rise a little but mainly for direction. The air rises at different rates as we glide over tidal shoals and deeper water, over the edge of the continent and out to deep sea. I am so strong, and so light. My mind is drinking every nuance of the land, the sea and the air. To our left the sky lightens as we reach an area of greater turbulence, fly through it and see ahead more land. The air steadies but now we are flying against the wind, beating up and gliding down to minimise effort. In the shallows we see fish, shoals of small fish shining in the clear water and the occasional larger, darker body from which they rush.

Suddenly my parents dive, back-wing at the last moment and rise, each with a silver fish in their feet. I sight on a shoal, drop and copy their example. My feet are in the water, I feel a cold body, close my talons and beat up towards the hilltop triumphantly bearing a not-very-large fish. I land beside my mother and hold the fish proudly beneath my foot in the scrub grass. Her fish is still squirming and she pecks its spine just behind the head. The body quivers and flaps for a moment then flops, still and dying if not dead. I copy but mine does not hold still. Two, three lunges with my comparatively smaller, weaker beak and finally it shudders as i hit bone and tear away. My father is further inland, tearing his fish into gobbets he swallows. Mother also gets into the serious business of feeding. As the sun warms my back I tuck into my first live kill, proudly. The future will hold many missed catches and possibly hungry days but today, my first lone hunt has given me the best tasting meal I will ever know.

The flycatcher

By Geraldine Paige

Authors note. This story is based on true events.

"Must keep my eyes open. Must keep my eyes open" Chanted Iain as he struggled to keep his eyelids from closing. Unfortunately Iain's eyelids won. But as it turns out it didn't really matter, because, when Sheila arrived back from her weekly Wednesday afternoon hair appointment, she ran straight upstairs into the bedroom. The noise of her opening and shutting drawers then banging about inside her wardrobe woke Iain up." Burglars" thought Iain. "Should I ring for the police or do I go upstairs".? Iain tossed a coin. "Heads. I go upstairs. But just to be on the safe side I had better arm myself. Now what can I use? Saucepan. Yes. Kitchen, here I come". With pan in his hot little hand, Iain silently tiptoed upstairs and made his way along the landing, until he found himself standing outside the bedroom door, counted to three then threw the door wide open. He went in waving the pan shouting. "GOT YOU". "Got what dear? And why are you waving my best saucepan about"? "I thought you were a burglar". "Burglar? But why?" "Because…". But before Iain had time to explain everything, Sheila interrupted him by saying. "You fell asleep and did not hear me when I came in." "But how did you know?" "Because I could see through the window that you were fast asleep." "But I could have been just resting my eyes." "NO. You were not resting your eyes because, my cup of tea in my favourite china cup and saucer was not ready and waiting for me"."But why didn't you wake me up?" "Because I wanted to sort out an outfit for tomorrow first." "Tomorrow. What's so special about tomorrow?" "The Bird Garden, remember?" "Yes. Sorry Sheila. Yes I do now. You wanted to take some photos for your talk at next month's W.I meeting. And of course have one of your wonderful picnics. But you still haven't answered my question, which was. What is so special about tomorrow? And before you say again about taking some photos, which you have done so many times before. You normally just take a dress out of the wardrobe, say, 'do you like it?' and before I have a chance to say anything, you would put it on, go downstairs, make up the picnic and off we would go.""I can see that you haven't noticed?" "Noticed what?" "My hair". "Yes, I know you've been to the hairdresser. And I know, that you know that you have been to the hairdresser". " I can see that I will have to tell you, because, if I don't, we will be here for the rest of the day going around in circles. I'TS THE COLOUR. I thought that I would have a change. As you can see I have chosen the wrong colour." Lost for words, Iain was down the stairs and into the kitchen so fast that he was almost flying. Sitting in the kitchen drinking tea, Iain suddenly came out with. "The reason why that I didn't notice, was because it looked so natural on you" "Nice try Iain. But really. BRIGHT RED. I ask you. But when it comes to the baloney, you pass with flying colours. Why didn't you just come out with it and say, I didn't notice?" Trying to make light of the situation Iain came out with. "Well you must admit, it's quality baloney." "Yes. I'll give you that" said

14

Sheila. "Now that we have sorted that out, it's back to. What do I wear?" "Sheila! I will tell you the truth. Just wear anything." "But what if the colours clash?" "So what. You never know you just might start a new fashion".

The following day Iain and Sheila turned up at the Bird Garden just in time to see a Falconry Display. Sheila was having a wonderful time taking photos, until she heard someone behind her, giggling. Do I turn around, or just ignore it? Thought Sheila. But, there again, why should I think that they are giggling at me?

"Those Falcon's were magnificent. If my photos don't win me a prize this year, at the W.I. I will be very surprised. Iain? Seeing that it's almost lunchtime, why don't we have our picnic by the lake."? "Yes that sounds nice. And they have a very wide variety of Water Fowl there that you can take some more photos of."

As Sheila was busily taking photos, she heard giggling, again. This time, she turned around only to see a group of people looking at her with their hands over their mouths, trying to muffle their giggles. " That's it. I'm right." said Sheila to herself "Now where's Iain?"

Finding Iain, she started to explain about the giggling. His reply was. "Now why would anyone be giggling at you? Now I'm a hungry man, feed me Oh great Wife of mine." With a bobbed curtsy Sheila's reply was" Yes. Yes. Oh Great Husband of mine".

Sitting back on the picnic bench patting his tummy Iain said. "That was a marvellous picnic". Still keeping their act going, Sheila went down on bended knee, bowed her head, clasped her hand's together, she then held them above her head, followed by her looking up at Iain with

15

pleading eye's and saying "I'm so happy that Oh Great Husband of mine was pleased". " That's very good dear. Now. I was thinking. And yes before you say anything, I have been eating my brain food. Exotic Birds". "I beg your pardon"."You heard. Exotic Birds. They are in the Wooded part of the grounds. And before you say. Are they flying about. No. They are not".

Unfortunately. The walk to the Exotic Bird section was some distance. "What a walk" said Sheila as she started to unbutton her blue cardigan. "I am boiling. Must sit down on that bench over there to cool off. I'll catch up with you later Iain" Sheila's sit down was not a very happy experience. The giggling stared up again. What is it with all of this giggling thought Sheila. Every time I sit down I hear people giggling. Ian keeps telling me I am imagining it. To Sheila's relief. This time she was right. How did she find out? The group of people that were giggling at her, were so close to her that when they passed by, Sheila was able to hear what they were saying. By the time Iain came back to see why she was taking so long to cool down. All he found was Sheila's shoulders going up and down to the rhythm of her sobbing, instead of a very refreshed Sheila.

"Now. Now. What's the matter?" "THE MATTER" Shouted Sheila. "I'll tell you what the matter is. Apparently I look just like the Union Flag.""Sorry Sheila, I just don't understand what you are on about." "That group of people that has just passed by me. I heard what they were saying." "Well yes, what did they say". "One of them said Oh look at the Red, White and Blue lady. Then another one said. She looks just like the Union Flag. And the awful thing is

Iain. They are right. Just look at me. Red hair, White dress and a Blue cardigan." By now, Sheila is nothing but a sobbing hysterical blancmange. Or should I say a sobbing hysterical Red White and Blue blancmange. "But--------
"No Buts about it Iain. I do look like the Union Flag."Iain tried again to say something in the hope that it would help to calm her down. But. Unfortunately all he could come up with, was. "Well what's wrong with looking like the Union Flag. The good old Red White and Blue?" A very stern. " IAIN. I think you have said quite enough. Now. The Exotic Bird Section, here I come with camera at the ready."

The moment Sheila laid her eyes on the Exotic Birds. The upset about the giggling and the Red White and Blue, was completely forgotten, her camera was clicking away like there was a no tomorrow.

"Names Sheila, names." "What are you talking about Iain?" "Names. Don't forget the names". "Yes. I know you said NAMES. In fact you said it quite a few times. But what about them?" "The names of the birds. It's all very well having photos of beautiful birds. But if you could put the names to them as well, your talk will be so much more interesting." "Yes. Thank you Iain. I had better get out my reading glasses".

Everything was going well, until Sheila came across a name plate that was just that little bit too far away to read properly. "It's no good Iain, I will have to find a way to get nearer. I must have that birds name. He is so magnificent. Just look at him with his long dark orange wings and tail, white head and grey body. I am going to climb over the barrier, so you had better keep a look out for me. Won't be

17

long."

In her enthusiasm to get the birds name, Sheila went just that little bit too near the aviary that the bird was in. In fact. Sheila was so close that her hair was touching the aviary wire. "Got it. It's called African Paradise Flycatcher. Ouch. What was that Iain? Ouch. There it goes again." By now Iain was laughing so much that he had tears running down his cheeks. "It's the bird" said Iain. "What are you talking about." "The bird. It's pulling your hair. He must like the colour". "Don't you start on about that again. And. It's all very well you thinking it's funny, but I cannot move, the bird has got such a strong pull, that I will have to cut my hair." Sheila was praying that she had her travelling manicure set in her handbag. "YES". said Sheila as she retrieved her nail scissors. "Come on Sheila get cutting before someone comes along." With a deep breath she started to cut her hair. Just to add to Sheila's problems, nail scissors are not designed for cutting hair. After what seemed an age, Sheila had to stop because her fingers were hurting her. "Sheila. Don't stop" With beads of sweat running down her face that is now the same colour red as her hair. Sheila gave her husband a look that said. If you know what's good for you, you, will keep your mouth shut. Finally, Iain heard the words. "I've cut myself free". "And not before time. The keeper is on his way. Get a move on." " Can't you distract him while I get my breath back"? "No I can't. Give me your hand and I will help you climb back over the barrier". With a lot of huffing, puffing and pulling Iain managed to get Sheila back over the barrier just before the keeper appeared. Sheila was now not only wearing a very interesting hair cut, but looking extremely dishevelled hot and bothered, and she was also very out of breath.   "What a beautiful bird", she said "Yes. The African Paradise Flycatcher is very popular. Well I must get on." said the keeper. "Hope you enjoy the rest of your visit."

The moment the keeper was out of sight Sheila and Iain breathed a sigh of relief. "I am surprised he didn't notice my lump of red hair in The African Paradise's break". "Well, just thank your lucky stars that he didn't. Now let's go home."

The Fish

By Nikki Pebble

Between the old railway bridge and chemical pipeline two teams faced each other across the river as it wound its way gently under the light of a violent blue sky. Reflections of the hard, hot sun made all the anglers squint toward a figure near the bridge, holding a red flag. A silence fell as even the native herons had decided it was too hot to fish today. Rods were held vertically at the ready. The red flag was raised. On the last stroke of midday the flag dropped and a dozen rods moved in concert like palm trees in a hurricane.

Mac McAnally had chosen his spot with care. He sat with his colour co-ordinated fishing gear under the shade of a weeping willow as he surveyed his 'honey pot' spot. For the last ten years he had competed in the village fishing competition, never to have won, but often quite close to the top spot. This time it would be different. All his new equipment was the best in the catalogue and he knew that he would be paying it off for years to come – unless he beat the local record - either for heaviest fish or highest number of catches. As long as he won, nothing else mattered. Anything that could help him was suitably employed, right down to his lucky red socks and batman y-fronts.

He surreptitiously glanced across the ambling river, looking for the absurd red hat that Tommy Jones liked to wear for competition. There he was, over to the left, sitting on an old bread basket. He didn't even have a decent rod, just an old wooden one that had obviously seen better decades.

"Ha!!" grunted a voice further off as the gentle water of the river was disturbed by the death fight of a small silver perch. The owner of the voice, a young, enthusiastic new barmaid from the Royal Hotel continued to fight for her trophy. She appeared to swell as the eyes of several of the local anglers were drawn to her unfeasibly long legs and media approved body.
Their lust sickened Mac, as he snarled in her direction, and immediately tried to hide it behind a half hearted cast, and a swig from his colour co-ordinated flask. Damned woman had only arrived in the village ten years ago – these newcomers were getting too full of themselves. He would show them and they, in their turn, would have to offer him some of the respect that he longed for.

Between the uncompromising sky and the pressure of match fishing, Mac finished his flask. He threw it none too gently into his colour coordinated fishing bag and began to chum the water with a mixture of cat food and a two day old egg mayo mix that he had found under the bins in the village car park.

Then the water roiled slightly as if something was feasting on his efforts, the float bobbed and a little later disappeared of its own accord. Mac staggered to his feet and jerked to line. His rod was bending much further than the picture in his catalogue showed. Had he caught a rock or some other sunken, waterlogged obstruction or…. Could it be…..this time…?

The surface of the water broke and for an instant he saw a spotted pattern body, large broad head, flattened snout and huge mouth full of sharp, backward facing teeth. At last, something worthy of his new equipment.

The fight began in earnest. The leviathan must be almost half his body weight. How proud he would be to show off this river monster. Maybe he would mount it and give it to the girl in the pub. That would show everybody his prowess, maybe even wipe the supercilious shit-eating grins from their faces. In his enthusiasm he grunted with effort. The eyes of the other competitors swung in his direction. He tried to arch his body to the shape of a socialist statue but his flab spoilt the effect.

The line went slack for just a brief moment as the large pike stopped to reassess its predicament, when suddenly, with a massive thrust from its tail, it took off toward the pipelines at the far end of the pitch. Mac was so busy reeling in that he was caught completely off guard and followed his colour coordinated rod into the water. The splash drew attention to his predicament just in time to hide the end of a broken shopping trolley that thrust up through his chest and impaled him like the mounted trophy. The pike surveyed its trophy, ate the eyes and part of the neck, before going home to show its mate.

Ella, The Secret Dragon

by Stephen Breakspear

Chapter One - C.A.T.S.

Skyla felt the heat rising around her eyes whenever she thought of her Daddy and that special day at the airport. Skyla had been so excited to be so close to the huge noisy aeroplane, with all those people in their smart uniforms just like her Daddy wore. She had been excited but all the big people, all the adults, told her that her Daddy had been in that large box with the large flag over it, and that she needed to be quiet and a good girl today, especially for Mummy. Skyla had noticed how pretty her Mummy had been on that day even though she was dressed all in black just like all the other people that were not soldiers.

She knew then, even at ten, but almost eleven, that she would never see her Daddy again. She knew that all she had left of him was her Mummy, and her little friend Ella that Daddy had given her as a kitten so long ago. He had said that Skyla was to look after Ella, just like Mummy looked after Skyla.

Skyla and Ella were playing at the bottom of their long garden down near the old orchard. They were near the tall fence that marked the end of their orchard and the start of the old factory building. Thick Bramble bushes grew up against the Factory fence where Skyla and Ella collected the fat blackberries that escaped into their garden more each year. Skyla did the blackberry collecting while Ella chased insects, or lay in the warm sun watching, and listening, as Skyla told off Ella for being so lazy.

Skyla had set to work collecting Blackberries in her bucket that she had used to take to the beach, while Ella, in a more energetic mood than normal, was chasing a slow moving bumble bee.

Ella jumped here, and leapt there, when she gave out a large angry hiss. Skyla ignored her as Ella would make often make noises like that while playing. This was different as Ella hissed again, and then made a sound that Skyla had not heard before. Ella was frightened, and Skyla could see the bush that hid Ella violently shaking and rustling.

Dropping her bucket of blackberries, Skyla ran over to the bush that hid Ella but she was quiet now except for mewling that sounded like "Help me." It may have not been in words but Skyla knew inside, somehow, that her friend, Ella, was crying out to her for help.

Dropping onto the ground to look into the gap she could see Ella stuck in an awkward Garfield pose with legs out in the air and a tail not moving, not lashing about. It didn't seem right that Ella could stay unmoving in that awkward position until Skyla saw very fine wires wrapped around Ella's body. They looked as if they should break because they were so thin but didn't. They just seemed to get tighter, and tighter, as Ella struggled less and less every passing second, until only Ella's frightened mewling was left to tell Skyla that she was still breathing just a metre away.

Searching for a way through to Ella she saw the bushes moving on the other side of the factory fence. Something was coming for her Ella, and Skyla knew she had to hurry to protect her just like her Daddy had said.

"Look after her Skyla, that's your job now, nobody else's. We expect you to look after Ella, just like Mummy looks after you. Can you do that Skyla, can you look after Ella, keep her safe?"

Skyla had to keep her promise to her Daddy because she loved her Daddy and she also loved Ella. Looking around, Skyla saw the old stick that she and Ella had played with many times. There was a leaf stuck on the thin end that she and Ella had pretended was a butterfly annoying Ella. It was so Ella could practise her 'play fighting' and her hunting skills. Daddy had told her that she should do that so that it would help Ella .... help Ella "develop".

Skyla jumped up, catching her arm on the brambles and scratching it deeply but she didn't feel it as she ran over to the butterfly stick. She ran back to the gap under the bush and threw herself to the ground so that she see through again. Whatever was coming toward Ella from the far side wasn't in any hurry but Skyla knew she didn't have much time. She had already worked out that she had to break the wires holding Ella or, she had to break the things that the wires were attached to; the bushes; the leaves: but how?

Where she held the stick at the thicker end she could see where she had broken off the smaller branches that had grown off it. Skyla knew if she pulled at the branches with the reversed stick then she would be able to hook the wires attached to the branches. She could pull off the wires and then she could drag the tied up Ella to her before whatever was coming, arrived.

Reaching in with the stick Skyla pushed the 'hooked branch' into the bush to Ella's side and pulled it back but it didn't catch on anything, just dislodged a few leaves. She had pulled too fast, and she hadn't turned it, she had rushed it.

Skyla worked the stick back in and concentrated on pulling the stick out slowly making sure that she was rotating it. Then, she felt it catch, she didn't know on what, but she continued pulling slowly and was rewarded with seeing the wires and the bush came toward her. She continued to pull until they stopped coming completely. Skyla wasn't as strong as her Daddy but she had the same determination, the same stubbornness that he had, so she kept pulling, straining, even though it was starting to hurt now. Suddenly, without any warning, it worked, her stick came free pulling just one wire free, but it had worked. Skyla spoke for the first time, "Ella, I'm coming, you'll soon be free. I'm on my way now, I won't leave you Ella, I won't leave you, I promise."

As she shouted to Ella, the rustling on the other side of the wire had stopped, but only for a while. It continued on again slower and almost, it appeared, more cautiously. As it moved forward the sound spread out sideways to each side. She could see now that the bushes were now moving in three very different directions, one toward Ella and two others going left and right of Ella. Whatever was coming was not on it's own, and had at least two others with it. The good thing was that they were going much slower now, so Skyla redoubled her efforts and started to break the wires that were higher up because she had worked out that if she broke these then Ella could fall backwards toward her leaving only the wires at the bottom. Then she could reach through and grab Ella pulling her through the gap and breaking the few remaining strands of wire. At least, that was her plan, until she saw what was hunting Ella.

A huge black hairy leg came through the bush on the other side of Ella, followed by two other legs, then a hairy body and she could see what it was, a very large spider, very large indeed. From what she could see in her cramped lying down position, it was at least the same size as Ella, but she also realised that she could not see it all yet and that she had stopped moving completely.

All she could do was look into it's two large eyes, but then she noticed the other smaller eyes, all looking directly at her and it looked really, really angry, especially when it moved its huge downward pointing fangs - sideways. Skyla had never been scared of spiders, because her Daddy had never been scared of spiders. He had told her that they keep the bad insects, like flies, away from houses and that they were probably more scared of us than we were of them. Skyla always believed her Daddy because she trusted her Daddy but she knew, instinctively that in this instance, that this spider definitely wasn't scared of her.. She still trusted her Daddy so on the other hand, Skyla wasn't scared of this spider either, just amazed at the size of it but then she saw the other two step out into the clearing either side of the first spider. They were not quite as big as the first one, but not by much, and they looked just as angry, if spiders can look angry that is.

The first spider continued to walk out into the small clearing, then around the wire trapping Ella and slowly advanced on Skyla, who was still lying on the ground, and still holding the butterfly stick. It was then Skyla realised that the stuff holding Ella wasn't wire but was a spider's web, from one of these in front of her probably.

As the big spider advanced toward her, Skyla moved backwards on her elbows and knees, just like her Daddy had made her practise at the beach last Summer. She kept hold of the stick in her right hand and moved quickly but not as quickly as the spider, but still, she was back out in the open before it came out from under the bushes. They both stopped, Skyla lying out flat and the spider raised up on it's back four legs.

It hissed, Skyla didn't know if normal size spiders could hiss but this one certainly did. Slowly moving up onto her knees and, still holding her stick, she stood up. The spider moved sideways, away from the hole, and then stopped. Skyla tried to watch it and to keep an eye on the hole, just in case the other two came out. From the corner of her eye she saw the spider drop down. Next second it was leaping at her face, with those wicked looking fangs, dripping some kind of thick liquid. Skyla ducked and the large spider flew past where she had been standing.

Turning on the spot she swung the stick just like she did at rounder's practise in school and she caught the spider in mid-flight. She felt the heavy, thicker end of her stick connect solidly with it as it suddenly changed direction in mid-air. The force of her blow had turned it onto it's back where it lay winded for a few seconds before twitching it's hairy legs in an attempt to get back on it's feet.

It was hissing even more loudly now but Skyla wasn't finished as it was her turn to launch herself at the spider. She swung her stick at the wriggling hairy black mass on the ground several times. The end of her make shift club was now covered in a yellow sticky liquid which was probably the creature's blood. Finally it stopped hissing and it's movements slowed down to an occasional twitch and Skyla could breathe again.

"Ella" she shouted and dived to the gap under the bush without a thought for the other two spiders that had been with the big one. Inside the bush, the two spiders and Ella had gone back through the fence surrounding the old factory unit. Skyla had promised her father that she would take care of Ella so she knew that keeping that promise outweighed her other promise to never go into the factory grounds. She knew that her father would understand and would agree. She also knew that her father would look over her and keep her safe as she found a way round to the hole in the fence. Taking her stick in her hand, she pulled the gap in the fence open and big enough for her to climb through. Pausing for a second she said quietly, "Ella, I'm coming, you'll soon be free. I'm on my way now, I won't leave you Ella, I won't leave you, I promise."

TO BE CONTINUED.......

The Dog Show

By Sally Ann Nixon

We've entered the village Dog Show. A real combination of Crufts and Scruffs. There are sections for working dogs, companion dogs, obedience, cuteness and the waggiest tail. Its felt that every dog in the village should fall under one of those headings, so the turnout should be good. There's loads of farmers with collies, the odd lurcher, children with cairns, yorkies and pugs, serious looking ladies with spaniels, Labradors and a gorgeous red setter.

We have entered Bella on her tail wagging ability and Tommy has gone in on his markings and gormlessness. Cute ? Maybe, but we doubt out it. All very casual, all very relaxed. No pooper scoopers at dawn here.

Oh. Wait. There's a last minute entry. A flustered looking lady, dressed in flowing black and green, towed by a large... what? Dog is certainly involved in its composition. Its big, a massive head and floppy ears like a cartoon retriever. It yawns, its ears flap and it reveals a jaw full of white pointed teeth , topped by cat like gold eyes set in its black furred head. Its long, red tongue lolls out and it sniffs the smells coming from the pig roast. So far, so dog. Its owner, Mrs Rhys, who runs the herbalist centre just outside the village and who can be a little odd, enters the creature as Brian, 2 years old and a cross-breed.

Brian sits and we realise that he has feet like a bird of prey. Talons , long claws,almost webbed at the top. Crinkled and hairless, they indent the mud. No sign of a paw print at all.

Brian is wearing a bright red coat. Mrs Rhys unfastens it anxiously.

"He isn't keen on the cold wind" and we gasp as two black wings unbind and rise softly into the breeze. Both Brian and Mrs Rhys float up gently and hover for a moment.

"Down, Brian", orders Mrs Rhys and they return just as gently to earth.

"He's very obedient, you see", says Mrs Rhys, hopefully. "No trouble at all".

The judges pause briefly to confer. They have seen many strange creatures over the years but this is something else...

Brian's tail emerges from between his back legs and he wags it enthusiastically, threatening to demolish the knitted toys and bric a brac stalls behind him.

That tail is certainly waggy. Its also lethal, with soft black fur to half way up then merging into scales to the end where it turns into a sort of arrow spike.

We all step back a bit. Brian shows a sort of puppy enthusiasm for play, towing Mrs Rhys towards a terrified Rottweiler.

Somehow she gets him under control.

"Sit, Brian, sit", tapping him with a hazel dowsing rod. It works and Brian subsides scratching one of his floppy ears.

One of the judges, an old man in tweeds, gathers his nerve and clears his throat.

"Er, Mrs Rhys. What breeds of dog would you say have gone into the making of Brian"?

He smiles weakly. Brian flaps his wings a little and preens. "Well, I'm not really sure. My Sukie - you all know Sukie my old retriever. She got out, she did, a few months back. When it was cold, like. Went for a sniff around, see, and when she came back , she looked a bit tousled. Stunned really. Gave her my arnica tonic. Set her up again, it did".

"Yes, but what is Brian. Half retriever we gather, but what is the other half"?

Mrs Rhys considered.

"Well theres a problem. I don't rightly know. We live under the mountain, see, and Sukie likes to go up to the cave there. No sheep to worry about and lots of nice smells for her. I go with her to collect the piles on the slope. Plenty of it and so good for the tomatoes. Not so nice after dark, you mind. Funny noises and huge bats, big as a cart horses they are swooping about. Oh, I wouldn't let her up there then".

The judge swallows and eyes up Brian,who rightly speaking, shouldn't exist.

Mrs Rhys shows a little defiance.

"He's mainly dog though, aren't you Cariad"?

She strokes Brian's head and he rubs his huge head on her shoulder.

"No one said he had to be all dog to enter the show".

The animal

By Jayne Hecate

The nest was warm, the usual security was gone and shaking with fear and confusion, the animal lay. Fur wet, eyes damaged, bones grinding in sockets. If the animal felt any emotion at all, it was only that of fear, the fear of predation, the urge to survive was strong, but fear and shock could and likely would kill it. No bigger than the span of the two hands that had hurt it, teeth and claws that had fought for survival, ached with the acid burn of exertion and exhaustion. The burning sting in the eyes would not end and the animal lay, shaking as the whole of its life became pain and suffering. A pain that it could not understand in the simple survival mind of a small mammal. It did not even whimper; to do so would attract predators, so in silence, the animal lay gently licking the blood from it's paws, washing it's face delicately to try to ease the pain in its dimmed eyes. Across the damaged surface of it's eyeballs, bacteria thrived, getting into every new crack and crevice of the lens. If the shock did not kill it, the infection might well do so. The saliva added a wetness to the animals eyes, a wetness that took away a tiny part of the pain, but gave the bacteria even more fluid to thrive and thrive they did.

Bernard sat back in his small office chair, sucking hard on the cigarette that he had stolen from his mother's packet, secreted away in her handbag. If she accused him of smoking, she would have to admit that she was smoking again and that was a battle that she did not want to lose. He blew a smoke ring, a trick that he had learned from his uncle. The secret was in the shaping of the lips and then the huff to push out the smoke in a careful ring; to float on the air, the hot smoke slowly rising in the warm stale air of the room. The room was just as a teenage boys room should be, with computer game magazines sat in a rough pile on the chest of drawers, but they were the sort of stack that was held up by console controllers while being supported by a clean t-shirt that his mother had left for him days earlier. The drawers in the unit hung open, the contents shoved in rather than folded, as they had been when his mother had put his clothes away in his younger previous years. The carpet was straw coloured, faded and filled with dust. Each week his mother nagged him to push the vacuum cleaner around his room, each week he promised that he would and each week he broke that promise as soon as she left the house, leaving him in the care of Uncle Colin who sat smoking and drinking down stairs.

The infection spread quickly, what sight the animal still had was soon fogged up with pus and slime as bacterial cells bred and died on the damaged surface of it's eyes. The natural response of the animal's immune system was to heat up, create a fever to kill off the bacteria, but it was not doing so well. With the increase in temperature, the animal grew thirsty, but the usual water supply had dried up. It had been dry for days despite the rainfall that fell at night. No longer crouched on its hind legs, it had curled into a ball, the desperately ill animal lay panting on its side. Fear at every noise, fine soft fur matted with perspiration, the infection actively running across its face, clogging its nose, the smell was putrid. The animal lay in its nest still and silent. Only the keenest of ears could have heard the sound of its breath.

When Bernard's mother left for work each evening for the night shift in the sandwich factory; where she toiled on minimum wage cleaning the lines and washing out the vats that the fillings were mixed in by the food processors; Bernard locked his door and on some occasions shoved the chair under the door handle. He hated being separated from his mother, but he also hated her company too. She tried to keep everything light, quietly pretending that everything was OK. Bernard's dad worked in Saudi, the manager of a golf course bar, where he had dated a woman who had worked the tables, cleaning away unwanted drinks and sweeping up dropped food from the floor. When not working in the golf club bar, the couple had retired to their cheap air conditioned flat, which due to local law was almost entirely alcohol free. Through his international contacts, they occasionally smuggled in a bottle of something special, a rare bottle of whiskey, or an expensive and exotic bottle of rum and that is how the twins had been conceived. Returning back to the cold of the UK had always been an option for him, but to do so with the woman he had got pregnant and the two children she had given birth too, would put him in a terrible place. So he endured the heat and the mindless chat of the golf course bar, where he earned a relatively comfortable wage. A European barman was after all, something of a gimmick and the golf club did well out him, just as he did well out of the tips of the men who drank their illegal drinks there. The sort of men who gave large tips to a white man who they could enjoy looking down on.

On the third day of the infection, the animal was completely blind, all that it could perceive was the vague shades of light and dark through the pus and dried fluids. Thirst burned its parched throat and every now and again, it would venture to the edge of its nest, desperate for a drop of water, but not even the smallest drop came. The chances of it surviving were slim, the fever, the infection and the thirst were taking all of the reserves that its tiny weak body had and they were starting to run out.

The door handle of Bernard's room began to twist, slowly and quietly at first. The chair held firm and the lock backed it up. Bernard blew smoke out of the window and prepared to fight. At fifteen he was almost a man, his back had grown strong and his fists were powerful when fighting boys of his own age or younger. Fighting off his new uncle was an impossible battle though, on some of the better days he gave back almost as much violence as he received, but on most days he did not. The door strained as his uncle put his shoulder against it and pushed hard. The top corner of the door almost came clear of the frame, but the flex and the improvised barrier held. The anger from the other side of the cheap wooden barrier was palpable and the next thrust was harder, cracking the door frame, giving it a long split that protruded sharp white splinters.

Dehydration, infection and fever had for a while sped the heart rate of the animal to a race, but now it was slow, almost lazy and the animal rested in painful sleep. It's tiny mind unable to comprehend the fact that death was near, that the suffering was almost over. Soon all sensation would stop and all of the pain would end, but the animal could not know this or it too would have wished for death, just as it's owner did, as he too lay in his nest, full of infection, full of pain and dying inside.

The broken remains of the chair were scattered across the carpet, the magazines strewn across the faded dirty carpet. Bernard lay in his bed, his soul empty, his body sore. He could not hear the dying animal in the small cage in his room. He could not hear the sounds of his uncle retreating back down the stairs, his steps fading as each one dropped lower on the stairs than the last.

The bluebottles found the animal in its rigid frozen state. The infection in its eyes dry, the last beat of its heart only hours before. The paws that had reached out for the water that never came, they had frozen in that position, frozen in rigid flesh. Glistening in the fur were the eggs of the flies, moist and slick as slowly they began to hatch into the wriggling mass of larvae that consumed the flesh of the animal where it lay. The smell of death was almost as bad as the smell of the maggots themselves. Even the boy in his bed of evil could smell them, but his mind was too broken, his body too sore to care.

When his mother came home, she opened the door and her

nose burned by cigarettes barely noticed the smell of death or the smell of the destruction of her boy. She flopped down onto the sofa where her boyfriend lay passed out, surrounded by the full ashtrays and the empty drink bottles. He made as much mess in her front room as he had of her boys soul. As she looked at him with disgust, her mind flashed with fear, he was all that she had and she must endure, they both must endure. He stirred slightly and roused himself enough to drop his arm over her, not in love or even passion, but in ownership. To move even a tiny amount would disturb him in his drunken slumber and that would result in a beating for her and maybe her boy too. Part of her felt it was what she deserved. Silently, she wondered if she could kill the man who owned her; but it was a momentary flash of fantasy across her idle exhausted mind. Life was not like that easy. No, life was cruel, life was only suffering and pain and all that lived, suffered and endured pain. All that suffered, all that felt pain, in the end, died in misery.

Bernard wept into his pillow, his Mother wept into her own elbow as she tried to put aside the pain of the uncomfortable position she found herself trapped in. The snores of the man next to her were the only sounds of peace anywhere in the house.

Walking with humans

by Margaret Ingram

The rain had stopped for now but the whole world was sodden. I quite enjoy this kind of weather for a walk since the scents are carried around easily and I can identify the recent passage of more animals than on dry summer days. I My human, Shelly, had got her waterproofs on, which made her very noisy, swishing with every step. Not really a problem for most of the walk, since I would be off the lead as soon as we were across the road at the top of the drive. Living this near the woods was a definite bonus. When we had been in the city I had been on the lead for ages before we reached the park, which was OK when Shelly was prepared to wait for me to scent the necessary information, but not on a cold or windy day when humans want to get on and keep moving. Poor scent-deprived mutants that they are, we have to make allowances for them but sometimes it is very hard not to snap!

In the woods that morning I was amazed to find out how many humans had been about already and realised that a great many of the trails, at least five individuals, were longer than usual. They all seemed to be about the same time, around dawn that morning so they were beginning to fade a little. Collecting information as I snuffled happily I realised that all had entered the woods at the same gate as us. They all followed the path although a couple of the trails were more alongside the main track then on it. I also found a few squirrels, being able to creep up on one and chase it up a Rowen nearby. Shelly was amused by that, which just shows how naughty we both are The squirrel swore at us from its perch high up above us. The local boars were at the farthest point of our walk, near the steep stream valley and off the human path by some distance. Shelly is good about letting me disappear for a few minutes without calling me back. Birds and all sorts amuse the monkey and keep them quiet, giving me the chance to stalk a little, honing my skills and occasionally startling wild foxes and food.

I digress. The tale of a normal walkies , the local monkey name for these hunts, is the setting for a more interesting happening, although nearly catching a passing stoat was amusing. Not every day one can creep up on a wild predator. Well, I say that but foxes and badgers cam be fairly easy to startle, especially one local fox who smells strongly of the human sources of its meals. Possibly it is a repatriated urban Renard, using our bins to save itself effort. She's raised several broods of cubs so it must work. I am still digressing.

I had, as I say, reached the boar territory's furthest extent, where it came closest to our normal route. It was an area of fairly dense undergrowth with ash and elders among the occasional oak and beech. Old and varied woodland, almost iconic in its depth and diversity. The scents were solikd and comforting, quintessentially countryside until I pushed through a bramble entanglement into a clearing about three lengths long and barely as wide. The wind was behind me so it was only as I got clear of the brush and leaves I got the scent. Then it grew until I could get nothing else. Monkey and dog guts and blood. I couldn't stop my instinctive howl. I just stopped and lifted my voice to the winds in a wolf-like throw-back to primeval hound. Humans call it belling I believe but I howled.

Shelley called and started coming towards me. I could hear their progress along the nearby track then they paused and started to crash through the undergrowth towards me. I stopped and knew I had to stop my monkey seeing this. They might even be able to smell it, because it was a mighty stink, overpowering even my rational mind. I rushed back towards Shelly and met them halfway into the surrounding thicket. They bent and cuddled me and kept up a continual barrage of questions as the inspected me for damage. 'Are you hurt? what's wrong? Oh, sweetie, why are you making that fuss? Show me!' On and on they ran, like true monkeys chatter whenever anything happens. They are worse than birds! I rubbed up against Shelly's legs and nuzzled the bits I could reach to reassure my dear monkey I was well, and unharmed. It is always heart-warming to know how much they care about my well-being, although I do believe some of that must be tied to their dislike of the vet, which seems almost as great as my own, and they don't even get a thermometer shoved up their arse routinely.

Finally Shelly calmed down and we started to fight our way through the brambles and saplings back onto the path. As we got to the path I got a strong whiff of one of the people who had been around the woods earlier, one of the ones I had scented. One of the ones who had been alongside the path more than on it! I didn't like this and felt my hackles rising. I clamped down on my instinctive growl. I didn't want to put this one on its guard.

We emerged and the stranger spoke to Shelly.

'are you all right? I heard the howling and your dash through the brambles. Do you need help?'

'No. Pooks is alright. I don't know what that was all about. Thank you for asking.'

'well, there are badgers and boars and all sorts of wildlife in these woods and I just wondered...'

'Thanks. We're fine. I'd better get Pooks home. We've done a couple of miles and it might rain again.' Shelly looked at the sky and started to move off. After a couple of steps they turned around and waved 'Thanks again', turned back and we kept going until the first bend in the path where we were out of sight of the stranger. Then they looked behind and stopped. 'I don't know what that was all about, they said rubbing my neck, 'but I did not like that stranger and I do not think they were offering help. They felt slimy!' I love Shelly. For a monkey, and a town-bred monkey at that, Shelly has instincts from our cave dwelling common past. I would even go so far as to suggest Shelly could probably survive with one of those cats or without a guardian at all!

They squatted down and, taking my head in their hands, stared into my eyes in that disconcerting way they do. I tried to show some concern then really did feel concern. I got a whiff of the stranger. I stood and pulled Shelly towards home and, bless the little darling, they came with not another word. We kept walking and speeded up as we went until we were trotting. After a good few minutes we neared the end of the woods. There was another stranger ahead, between us and home. I could smell their presence before we saw them. Another of the scents I had already got! Possibly a herd member with the one who had spoken to us or of the dead, gutted one. No way to know which. What to do? Give no clue we knew, don't engage. I tried to will Shelly to give a friendly, ordinary signal and once again the mental bond delivered. A bright "morning' , a smile, and we were up to and past the monkey. Seconds later we were out of the woods. There were two cars parked in the entrance but that wasn't unusual. Nonetheless Shelly had her phone out as we slowed to a sedate walk and captured the two images without letting anyone behind us see what was happening. Luckily neither car had anyone in it so we were probably safe. I thought we were going home but Shelly was not. We turned left and walked toward the village's main street. At the next gate Shelly looked around and, seeing no-one, which I could confirm by scent, led us into the woods again.

We set off and turned along a track which would take us over the stream and then we could head back towards the other track and the clearing and the strangers. Shelly was investigating! Yet there could be no scent-based mystery pushing this enquiry. Shelly had the instincts of a nose-blind wolf!

We quietly approached the clearing near the boars from the other side of the stream which would not be a real barrier in itself. I could leap across easily and I was pretty sure Shelly could, too. We could hear something going on long before we got there and I could smell the strangers and the guts being wafted our way. That was good, because it meant we were down-wind of them and any little noise we made would be hidden in the rustling of the woods and the animals noises. Sight is a poor primary sense in woods! Poor monkeys.

Shelly finally crept behind a fairly large poplar and peeked around it. The strangers could just be seen digging in the clearing, as close to the brambles as possible and not too far from us. Then they stopped digging and walked across towards the path, stopped, bent down and a stench of gut hit me. I couldn't stop the growl completely but the wind direction and poor monkey senses saved me from telling them we were here. Shelly's hand came down on my muzzle and 'Shhh!' quietly as if I needed it . I gave the monkey acquiescent signal by moving my head up and down. Sight signal again but one I could copy. We watched them half-carry, half drag something big and heavy towards us and the hole they had dug, dump it in and cover it, filling in the hole and then strewing it with leaves and stuff to make it look as normal as they could. It was not a good job of camouflage but they were monkeys so one must make allowances. The stench had been spread all over the place in this process so hunters would have been more confused than humans. The strangers left, carrying a couple of digging tools and we waited until they were away before retracing our steps and making it to the second gate in time to see one of the cars we had photographed

We waited and then walked into the village and ended up at Cello's kennel, sitting in the kitchen with Shelly chatting to one of Cello's humans, Cem. I liked Cem and agreed that they were indeed a gem, playing with their name. Evidently Cem's home pack were fare to the south-east and in a much hotter land. Cello had no idea where exactly but Cem sometimes talked of hunting with Hawks in the hills around his birthplace. Cello wasn't the brightest pup in the litter but she wanted to run free in the wilderness he described. Me, too!

Shelly told Cem what they knew but of course hadn't had all the information I had. I wondered how I could let her know about the scent info I had. No ideas came to me but perhaps Shelly and Cem would guess. They ended by Shelly phoning someone. The two of them agreed to meet whoever at the gate into the woods and we all got out of the village and up to the gate within a very short time. The rain was heavier and there were occasional rumbles of thunder. Cello was not a happy bitch and kept stopping to shake out the rain. Mind you, I was glad I was short haired in this weather. My guard hairs were slick but the undercoat was impermeable and I was fairly comfortable as long as we were moving. We stood at the gate for a few moments and then I heard a wailing in the distance. My ears pricked and I stood and Cello pointed at it a second later then the two humans took our hints and turned towards the main road. A car and van both wreathed in flashing lights screeched to a halt in the parking space and lots of humans emerged quickly. One came towards us and asked Shelly a series of staccato questions, listened to the answers and then turned to the others, spat a series of instructions to his pack leaders who passed orders down. The general pack set off in various directions and soon the area was taped off with plastic tapes and signs went up to warn humans away. We all went into the woods with the pack leader and two of his aides. We were soon nearing the clearing and one of the aides, using her communicator, ordered a second cordon set up. We continued into the clearing. I showed them where the smell was strongest, where the stuff had been buried and Shelly told the pack leader, Inspector, what I was showing them. More orders produced three humans in strange clothes with digging tools and tool boxes who started to remove the dirt. I tried to help but was dragged away by Shelly. No fun, these humans. I went over to where the stuff that was buried had been dragged from by the strangers and tried to get Shelly to understand how important it could be. Cello, clever bitch, started snuffling and found some spectacles which she gave to Cem, They called Inspector and after some fairly heated words, we were all moved away but the funnily-dressed humans split and one started looking where I had shown them.

After that nothing much happened except the usual monkey noise and to-and-fro-ing. Weeks later Shelly was called to a very interestingly scented building in the nearest city. I accompanied them and we saw a line of humans which included the first stranger we had seen that morning. I knew him instantly and growled. Shelly told Inspector what I meant.

Months later we moved here and Shelly was now called Charley

49

and I was called Ivan. I don't know what happened to Cem and Cello. But here we are and the local woods are fine. It is warmer here but no-one hunts with hawks that we know, I still don't understand why that walk changed everything, really. After all if humans didn't want one to kill another then they would stop using cars and get back to walking everywhere.

MR OWL AND MS PUSSYCAT

By Nim Mangat

I looked at her reclining upon a silken cushion and yearned to say a thousand beautiful things. Things I should have said before. Pussycat glanced at me from behind her fashionable sunglasses just for a moment and looked away, across the calm blue ocean at something in the distance. 'Mr Owl, we are moving further and further away from the shore –I can only stay until midday. Mummy and daddy are expecting me for lunch.' 'Of course, dearest. Why so formal. You can call me Tawny, there's no one for miles.' How was I going to explain that I'd prepared a picnic for the two of us. The best caviar that her father's money could buy. And pickled herrings, strawberries and cream. And Champagne , only the best of course. After months of intricate planning, telling her was just a minor hitch. I knew, without a doubt that Pussycat loved me, she just didn't know it yet. She was by nature, coy, guarded, cautious, but I had also seen a rebellious side to her. The night I serenaded her, under cover of darkness, lit only by the twinkling stars, when she was out on her balcony having an illicit smoke. She looked below, searching for the source of the beautiful music and then, she just smiled, removed her robe and let it drop, revealing her perfect feline form, silhouetted against the silvery moon. She blew kisses again and again and then disappeared inside. I am certain she knew it was me. This gave me a proud confidence I did not know I possessed. I puffed up my silky, feathers and stood up straight. I was in love and she knew I existed. I began

51

to hide notes where I knew only Pussy would find them. At first, she did not respond but I am tenacious by nature, I never give up. My friends say this is my gift and also my curse. I disagree. I remind them, it is precisely because of this gift that I now find myself in a privileged position. I am wealthy, I am about to ask for the hand of the most beautiful creature on the planet. I have my eye set on a seven bedroom, eight bathroom detached property in a salubrious part of Brookmans Park, good schools nearby, you know, for the children. My friends had gasped. Children? You two? They would be an abomination to society. You must cease this madness at once, they urged. I had always known my friends were envious of my success. I'd seen the way their eyes sparkled in the moonlight when I told them of my adventures with my darling Pussycat; all they could manage was an escape from the missus and their brood for five minutes, if they were lucky. They lived in appallingly crowded conditions, usually a one room tree apartment. I felt sorry for them, if truth be told. So, when Pussycat's nanny Cecille found one of my notes, she threatened to reveal all to her father, unless this relationship was ended immediately. I had to think fast, before all my hard work unravelled before me eyes. I had cried as I clutched Pussycats final note to my breast. Dear Mr Owl, the note read, we can meet one last time. To say goodbye. Otherwise Cecille will tell my father all. He will kill you if he ever finds out. She ended the note with a very formal Mademoiselle Pussycat. No kisses. My heart shattered into a million pieces. I was a poor honest soul. Her father cheated all his employees by not providing decent basic salaries, bonuses, fringe benefits. As I worked in the Finance Department of his successful haulage business, I had been able to squirrel away a little money every now and then and had built up a nice little nest egg. Mind, it's money I should have received by ways of annual pay rises Christmas bonuses etc. and I never took more than I felt was appropriate, only what I felt I was worth. So, over the last few years I have become an owl of means. Worthy for the hand of my employers only daughter. My darling responded to my letter when I advised my dearest of my intentions to ask for her hand in marriage, thus was her response, 'Are you mad? she wrote, Papa will kill you without hesitation. He will rip out your feathers, one by one and stuff them into an Ottoman for his feet. No! We must end this at once. Please do not destroy my reputation with your impossible dreams.' So brutal appeared her letter, my breath stopped midway in my chest, I felt I could not breathe, I was about to die, and then I hooted like a demented owl, cursing my body, my feathers, my beak, my wings. Oh why was I not born a handsome cat! Life was so unfair. I immediately replied we must have a final rendezvous in the Marina outside Costa next Sunday morning. As it was mid-summer and promised to be warm, I had in mind a little sailing trip. Pussycat was thrilled that I had seen sense. She came on Sunday, dressed in a fine silken gown and an enormous wide brimmed hat, finished off with a jewel coloured pheasant tail feather. She was a vision of perfection. 'This will be a perfect farewell,' she meeowed joyously. With a sunken heart, I helped her into the rented cruiser. I started the engine and when we were out a significant distance, set the course. The morning was pleasantly warm, without a cloud in the sky. The seagulls squawked maniacally. We chatted about the marvellous weather. She explained about her father and his strict rules. She smiled sweetly at me as she purred how we could move on with our lives and she accidentally on purpose mentioned a fellow from her circle of

53

close friends who was doing 'so well in business' and 'had shown an interest in her'. I clenched my beak tightly; I could never move on. I had found the only one I wanted to spend my life with forever. I fought back hot tears when they threatened to escape. 'Tawny, when are we turning back, surely it must be past midday now?' Pussy asked demurely. 'Sorry, my love, I don't have a watch, but I do have a little picnic prepared just in case we were feeling peckish.' I produced the basket of goodies and laid it out in front of her – she pecked delicately at a pickled herring. I bought out my ukulele and began to play 'Somewhere over the Rainbow' just as I had done one moonlit night under her balcony. 'Please stop the racket while I'm eating,' she said with her paws over her ears. Disappointed, I put my instrument away, agreeing it wasn't the same without the moon and the stars. 'My love, Pussy my love. You are the length, the breadth ....' 'I have no idea what you are on about,' she interrupted, in between mouthfuls of a luscious strawberry dipped in cream. 'You are the length, the breadth, the depth of my life. Without you, I am nothing,' I continued to recite from my specially crafted poem, just for her. My love smiled sadly, as she leant back into her silk cushion and sipped champagne from a crystal flute. 'Do we have enough fuel to return to the shore?' She asked. 'We are not going back to the shore, my sweet, we are sailing to France.' Just then I heard a noise in the distance. It was getting closer. 'Oh Tawny, daddy's sending his helicopters. I tried to tell you loads of times, there can never be 'us'. We are just too different.' Blood drained from my body – had I been a fool? I took hold of the controls, and the boat thrust forward at force. My advanced sailing course was worth every penny. The cruiser zig zagged dramatically as it cut its way through the limitless ocean towards France. If there was one thing I was certain of in my life, it was that I would never give up on my dream, because without it, what was left? Who would I be?

Day Out

By Geraldine Paige

Authors note. This story is based on true events.

"Four down. Clue. Makes noise?" Iain sitting in his favourite arm chair, was tapping the side of his face with a pencil trying to concentrate on his crossword. "No. Can't get it." Tries the next one. "Seven across. Clue. Go's with mash and gravy? Ha Ha. Yes. Got it. Sausages."
"Iain?". shouted Sheila as she came running into the front room where Iain was still trying to finish his crossword puzzle. "Our Spring bulb's ." "Well Sheila, what about them?" "Something has been eating them." "Got it". "Got what?" Inquired Sheila. "Four across". "Four across what? A road?" "No. My crossword. Four across. Makes noise". "And what is the answer?" With the innocent smile of a new born baby, Iain looked his wife Sheila straight in the eyes and said the answer was Wife . Trying to control her temper, Sheila said through gritted teeth. "THE BULBS. Something has been eating them." Iain now knows that he is walking on dangerous ground. Trying to lighten the atmosphere by (what he hope's will go down as a joke) said. "Well my sweet. It wasn't me. Ha Ha". The reply was a very sharp toss of the head, accompanied by loud sniffing as if one was trying to hold back tears. The drama, was then finished off by her stamping out of the room, and slamming the door as she made her way back to the potting shed. "Well apart from the interruption from Sheila, I think I have finished my crossword in record

time". said Iain as he was looking at his watch. But unfortunately not enough time for herself to cool down. What's on the telly?"

Iain woke up and looked at his watch. The blood immediately drained from his face." Dam and blast. Better get the peace offering ready (a cup of tea in her favourite china cup and saucer). Because if I even think about entering the war zone (the potting shed) without one, I will be in even more trouble".

By now the potting shed was almost shaking with fear to the sound's of Sheila voice saying." half eaten bulbs in the recycling, good one's in the wooden box. And. Where is my peace offering? He's late".

The next door neighbour , on hearing Sheilah, thought to himself Iain will be asking for tea and sanctuary if he does not get a move on. Better get the kettle on."

Luckily the the tea and sanctuary were not needed. Iain arrived with the peace offering just before the final scream. "Thank you Iain. But I am going indoors now." "But why?" " Because I am exhausted." Iain, now left holding the cup of tea in her favourite china cup and saucer, sits down on garden bench and drinks it. Wipes his mouth with the back of his hand, then says. "By- Jove. I do make a good cuppa". Then goes indoors to make Sheila another one. Only to find her lying down on the settee with the back of her hand pressed against her forehead. "It must have been all that shouting at the bulbs that exhausted her, poor little things. Yes I can feel a new saying coming on. BULB SHOUTING. That it. BULB SHOUTING. So when, or if she starts again, I will say. Are you BULB SHOUTING my sweet. Then stand back."

58

"Now that I have your un-divided". Said Iain "This leaflet has just been delivered advertising a new Garden Centre. Want to look at it?"Sheila still lying down in her dramatic pose said with a sigh."You read it to me, I am still too tired." Iain trying to keep a straight face cleared his throat then started to read out loud. "Everything for the Gardening and Steam Train enthusiast."

All of a sudden Sheila had forgotten about her drama, and was now sitting bolt upright wearing a very large grin on her face. "Steam Train's. Did you say Steam Train's?" "Yes. But there's more.". "Like what Iain.?" "Ornamental Garden's and a Cafe." "Really. How nice, we could have a snack at the Cafe, a walk around the Garden's buy our bulbs, then finish off with a lovely Steam Train ride. Yes that's it. Tomorrow is now sorted. This year I was thinking of making our grand children's Birthday and Christmas cards, with picture's of Steam Train's." "Yes Sheila. That's a good idea, it will be something personal and very different."

The following afternoon found Iain and Sheila standing on the platform waiting for the Train to arrive. "Sheila. Quick. The Camera. Train's coming". Click. "Got it. Thanks Iain." As the Train slowly came to a halt, it hissed out a very large cloud of steam." I am just off now to take a few photo's at different angles. Wont be long." Said Sheila

"Please do not board the Train" said the Driver, as he made his way to the engine shed. Meanwhile Sheila was so engrossed in her photography, that she was completely unaware that the train that was now standing at the platform, was driverless.

"Bother. I've taken too many photo's I have flattened my

batteries. Iain". Shouted Sheila. As she was now at the other end of the platform. "Have you got any spare batteries"? Iain, just gestured to her to come down to him. As Sheila was making her way down the platform towards her husband, she notice that the Train was standing there completely empty. "Iain.?Why is everyone just standing there and not boarding the Train? " "Of course ,you were not here, you were busy taking photo's. And. No. I do not have any spare batteries." "But what do you mean, I was not here?" Just as Iain was about to answer her, the Driver emerged from the engine shed accompanied by an Engineer, they both walked over to the driver's cab had a good look in. "You see what I mean!" said the driver. "Yes. You will have to give everyone their money back. Your tuppence ha-penny glass on your water gauge is cracked. And I do not have a spare one." Sheila overhearing the conversation open her handbag and brought out her powder compact. Then gave it to the Train Driver saying. "Young man. I overheard your conversation. The only glass I have with me is in this compact of mine. Unfortunately, I do not know how much it cost, because I bought it sometime ago, but you are very welcome to it." Then handed it over to a very confused looking Train Driver.

Silence. Absolute silence, that seemed to go on forever. Then was finally broken by the Driver saying. " Sorry Madam. I don't understand." A slightly annoyed Sheila's reply was. "Your cracked glass! You know. The tuppence ha-penny glass, the one with the water problem." Again. Silence. A very long silence.

"Well?" asked Sheila as her hopeful smile was just about

to disappear. Clearing his throat, and at the same time trying to keep a straight face. The Driver had finally worked out what had happened. "I think that you must have misheard me Madam." "Well. I assure you young man, that, for my age I have very good hearing." By now the Driver was finding it very difficult not to laugh . Clearing his throat for the second time, then bracing himself before saying. "The Toughened Safety Glass on the water gauge is cracked. Not Tuppence Ha-penny Glass".

Eddy and the biscuits

By Stephen Breakspear

Eddy opened his eyes, slowly. He was lying on his back, looking upwards and he had no idea why he was there. All that he could see around him in the darkened room was a table towering above him like a Manhattan skyscraper. As he hauled himself upward by clinging to the leg of the table the room presented itself as an old log cabin that was long unused. This was confirmed by the dust layer that he could make out as his eye level rose up past the table top, and if secondary confirmation was needed, he now became aware of the musty smell of the darkened room.

As his senses cleared, and while he waited for his strength to return, he noticed that on the table, in fact dead centre on the table, was a plate of what appeared to be brightly coloured iced ring biscuits. Six equally spaced biscuits that appeared to be fresh, or at least recent, as they were not covered in dust. What was intriguing was the contrast between the apparent antiquity of the room and the biscuits, obviously placed there meticulously, and specifically, to attract his attention once, and only if, he was standing.

Not wishing to stay in there any longer than he had to, and not without a little trepidation and effort, Eddy raised himself upright and walked around the table toward the only door in the room, reached down to the handle and opened the door towards him. Fully expecting it to be locked and pleasantly surprised that it was not, Eddy's elation turned to horror once he saw what was waiting for him on the other side of the door.

Between him and what appeared to be the only door to freedom, was a living carpet of rats that spread from wall to wall. This carpet moved much as a flock of birds moves with each individual responding to their neighbours' movements so forming little ripples and groundswells as the rat gestalt became a living, breathing entity before his eyes.

There was no doubt that he was expected to cross the floor of rats in order to leave, and that this was a test that had been set for him by others unknown, at least at present. He suspected that he would find out who had set this up once he passed through the opposite door.

The biscuits! Obviously he was to use the biscuits to assist him in crossing the floor, but how? Of course, these rats are probably hungry, and not a little annoyed at being penned up for some time. If he were to throw a biscuit into the rats then they would fight each other for the food clearing a partial way through, but he had six biscuits and about six meters to cross. Voila, he could throw a biscuit at six one metre spacings to one side of the room, the rats would rush over to one side and a path will clear allowing him to walk unimpeded to the exit. What a plan, but really he had Jason and the Golden Fleece to thank as that's how Jason single-handedly defeated the army of the dead spawned from the Hydra's teeth, thank God for his love of reading!

Or he could try something else, another method that didn't involve biscuits no matter how tasty, or fresh, they looked. Instead he just strode across the floor brushing the rats aside as if they were not of any concern to him which of course they weren't as rats did not bother him in the slightest and never had. He arrived at the opposite door without incident and even stood there calmly for a minute as he looked back at the rats that were milling about like water finding it's own level after a large rock had been dumped into it. He smiled to himself at the success of his own bravado and the simplicity of his plan. He even had his hand on the doorknob ready to open the door and leave, and was still smiling when the first rush of the rat swarm hit him covering him from head to toe. He was covered so effectively that there was no sound heard outside the room, but Eddy was screaming, but fortunately for Eddy the screaming didn't carry on for long and, fortunately for the rats, they weren't hungry any more.

The girls

By Jayne Hecate

Ida Ball was a little girl of nine, she had long strawberry blonde hair that fell past her shoulders and all the way down her back and if she leaned her head back as far as she could, she could sit on her own hair. Her pale green eyes stared out of freckled sockets in a friendly, oval face at her best friend Hillary Frank. Hillary was very slightly older than Ida by a week and a half. Hillary was also, as she explained proudly, half Nigerian on her Father's side. As such, Hillary had a mane of jet black hair that framed her delicate face from which she looked at the world with deep brown eyes. Ida and Hillary lived in the same street, a few houses apart, as well as attending the same school and the pair of them were inseparable throughout the summer holidays, playing together almost everyday.

On the fifth of September, the school term started once again and the girls were driven through the pouring rain to school by Hillary's father, in his brand new car. The car was a large electric thing with bright blue paint and funny top opening doors for the girls to climb out of. The autumn term was the last one that they would spend together in primary school, before moving up to secondary school the following year and it was with a familiar ease that they walked through the school gate together, having been waved off by Mr Frank.

The trees that surrounded the playground were already turning a rich golden yellow and dropping their leaves and even a few spiky chestnut cases to ground. Some of the other children in the playground were shrieking and scooping up armfuls of the leaves and throwing them at each other in fun, others were gathering the chestnuts from their cases, but Ida and Hillary had an entirely different game to play. Hillary's father had been reading exerts to them from his latest Andy McNab novel and the two girls were fascinated and enthused by the idea of their being in the SAS, having heard tell of the exciting adventures that the SAS soldiers had gone on. During his readings, Mr Frank had been careful not to read out too many gory details, much to the disappointment of the children. However, they had been amazed to learn that in the early days, the SAS had used bright pink jeeps in the desert and had trained to kill a man with their bare hands. So their games together often involved them sneaking up on each other and performing pretend surprise kills on each other from behind. The deaths were always protracted and very dramatic, often the amusement of the the killer as they watched their victim cough, shake and collapse to the ground. Some of the other parents had muttered about it not being appropriate for girls to play such games, but Mr Frank had told the girls that they should be true to themselves and should live their lives as they saw fit. He had spoken at length about them not giving into the ideas pushed onto them by many people that girls could only push prams or like baby dolls. As such he had ensured that his daughter not only had various types of dolls, but she also had plenty of toy cars, a big box of Lego, a couple of toy machine guns and Mr Frank had even donated one of his hankies to the girls to pretend was an ether soaked cloth to knock each other out.

At the end of their first week of the autumn term, Ida's parents had asked Mr Frank to collect Ida from school and then have her to stay with his family for the weekend. The two women had supplied fresh school uniform for their daughter for the following Monday, but the girls were very excited to have a whole weekend together with a sleepover. The weekend had been carefully planned out. On Saturday Ida and Hillary were going to learn to bake cakes with Mr Frank, who it was well known was an excellent chef. Then on Sunday the girls were going to go look in the tidal pools for sea animals with Mrs Frank, who worked as a scientist at the university and was an expert in such things.

Mr Frank led both girls from the school gate back to his car and once they both were all secure in the back with their seat belts and he had given each of them a packet of crisps to stem post school hunger, he started to drive out onto the busy road. It took only a few minutes for the girls to notice that they were not going back home and almost as one, they began to question Mr Frank as to where their destination. He grinned in the mirror and said that it was a secret that he could only tell them on pain of death and the girls giggled excitedly.

After half an hour of struggling through slow moving traffic, Mr Frank drew the car into the large car park outside the cinema and parked in one of the bays set aside for electric vehicles, with a charging station. The two girls were by now very excited as they climbed form the car and then hand in hand wandered towards the brightly lit building, just ahead of Hillary's father who smiled fondly as the girls skipped along happily. He bought the tickets and then as a happy chatty group, they went to get the popcorn, where he chose the biggest bucket he could get and three small drinks.

There was still a few minutes before the theatre was cleaned and ready for the next film and they could go in and find their seats, so Mr Frank sat down on a hard, colourful sofa to check his phone, while the girls wandered around the large waiting area and examined the posters for new movies still to come.

The screen on his phone suddenly lit up just as he was about to slip it back into his coat pocket, and he checked it already certain of what it was going to say. Ida's Mothers had spoken to the marriage counselor and it was decided that they were to go ahead with the separation and then begin the divorce. He sighed sadly despite knowing that it had probably been inevitable, but it was news that Ida did not need to hear right away and he switched off his phone away, slipped it back into his jacket pocket and called to the girls to get ready to go into the theater to find their seats.

'Fly on the Wall' meets Miss Prissy

By Jan Housby

"Good morning viewers. Today is the day we have been anxiously awaiting for at 'Fly on the Wall'. It is the first day of Spring. Traditionally, the VIPs (or Very Important Pets) emerge from their winter dwellings (the duvet). Our roving reporter, Alan Twit-Thistle, has been encamped outside 202 Blenheim Place, Canvey Island in the hopes of catching a glimpse of Miss Prissy, the exotic Persian Blue cat. We will go to Alan in just a moment, but first some background to the story."

Angus Merryweather swung his chair round and dramatically stared into camera two to begin the morning's scoop. "Prissy, as she is known to her closest friends, had a meteoric rise to fame last year after a random appearance on TOWIE. For the uninitiated, this stands for the drivellous but inexplicably popular TV show, 'The Only Way is Essex'."

Angus, the consummate professional, was aware of the producer yelling in his ear to stop slandering the reality show, but chose to ignore it. He continued his tour de force, "Prissy had experienced an urgent call of nature that day, and had been forced to step outside the cat flap. Sleepily she had dug a hole and squatted, tidied up after herself and then crawled back through the cat flap in order to go for another snooze on her feather duvet."

Spinning around again, Angus stared dramatically into

camera one, continuing with the story. "Of course, this would have been nothing out of the ordinary. Except for one strange twist of fate that day. TOWIE was being broadcast live for the first time. As the viewers settled down to watch Sharon and Tracey having their weekly cat-fight over Darren the Unreliable, the camera man had zoomed in on what he thought was a giant ball of grey fluff blowing about in the breeze. As the lens came into focus, what appeared was the most beautiful long-haired cat squatting over a hole, with a look of utter peace and bliss on her face. Her eyes were closed in meditation, unaware of the peeping-tom filming her morning ablutions. By the following morning, 'Prissy does a pissy' had scored over ten thousand hits on You Tube, being the most interesting thing that had ever happened on TOWIE. And thus, a star was born."

Angus, momentarily fantasising that this could be a BAFTA winning interview, swung his chair aggressively to the right and stared directly into camera three, making the cameraman jump. "So, Alan Twit-Thistle, has there been any sign of movement through the cat flap this morning?"

The screen suddenly flipped to show Mr Twit-Thistle, dressed in combats plus green balaclava, unsuccessfully trying to hide his gangly frame and handlebar moustache behind a lamp post.
"No", said Alan, dejectedly, feeling cold and miserable. "The two human servants went out at 8am as usual, but no sign of Miss Prissy as yet. Mind you, it is only 10.30am and we know how she likes her lie-ins. She will have had

breakfast by now though and her fur brushed".

"Ah, breakfast", Angus exclaimed, seizing immediately on a matter of major public interest. "Do we know what Miss Prissy might have eaten so far?".

"Well", garbled Alan breathlessly, "I had an opportunity to rummage through the rubbish yesterday, and it appears Miss Prissy has a possible addiction problem. There were seven, I repeat seven, empty packets of Cravers, the delectable treat cats allegedly can't resist!"

Angus at once put on his serious face, reserved especially for dramatic headlines. "Cravers, eh? I know it's legal, but that's dangerous stuff. The vets have been warning for years that overuse of organic catnip could lead a susceptible cat on to stronger synthetic drugs such as this. There is also the added complication of weight gain and a refusal to eat natural foods such as mice and rats".

Angus, again glaring intently into the camera, announced in his most serious voice, "Viewers, if this story raises concerns about your pets, please do call in to our help-line. We have a team of experts ready to give advice. The number should be at the bottom of your screens now. In the meantime, let's go back over to you, Alan".

Alan looked startled, but not this time by Angus. He was staring into the air whilst trying to shoo away a wasp that had become mesmerized by his jam sandwiches, which had unhelpfully stuck to his fingers. Just at that moment, the cat flap opened and out came Miss Prissy, in her finest diamond and ruby gold collar. At precisely the same time,

Alan started flapping his arms in the air, which further antagonized the wasp buzzing furiously around his head. Miss Prissy instantly became fixated on the insect and also this rather odd human who was apparently trying to fly like a bird, and seized the opportunity to show off her prowess as a hunter. To the horror of the director, a chain of events steamrollered into action.

Like a grey, fluffy phantom possessed, Miss Prissy ran at the speed of light, arriving suddenly at the feet of the cameraman, who was urgently trying to untangle yards of cables which had got caught under Alan's feet as he hopped around. To Miss Prissy's eyes, following her morning hit of Cravers, all she could now see was a tangle of snakes which needed taking out immediately. The snakes appeared more colourful and wiggly than ever before, poking their tongues out and hissing suggestively at her. In one seamless, simultaneous act, the wasp stung Alan on the cheek, who let out an enormous yelp. In the background, the cameraman was heard to scream, "Don't bite that, you stupid f...ing cat", followed by a fizzing sound and then blackness. It also signified a symbolic and sudden end to Angus Merryweather's flagship documentary programme, 'Fly on the Wall'.

* * * * *

Angus Merryweather never really recovered from the live broadcast on that fateful day, either mentally, spiritually or career-wise. Once the fur-balls had stopped flying, a documentary to the memory of the casualties was broadcast, entitled, "A day in the life (and death) of Miss Prissy, Alan Twit-Thistle and 'Fly on the Wall'." If only Miss Prissy hadn't been wearing her diamond and gold collar - it was unlikely that she would have survived the electric shock as she chewed through the camera cables onto the wet grass, but the metal collar hadn't helped matters. As for Alan, his allergy to fur along with a particularly nasty reaction to the wasp sting proved a fatal combination. They had attempted to rush him to Essex General Hospital, but had got stuck in a traffic jam on the A127. Further complications arose when they were unable to find a parking spot, compounded by the fact that they then didn't have enough money to pay the extortionate parking fee. Poor Alan gasped his last at the entrance to the steps to A & E, which had proved very difficult to find. The receptionists in the portacabin were somewhat irritated by the inconvenience - why were there never any porters around when you needed them? The nursing staff and doctors, whilst sad, were privately relieved that they were saved from yet another emergency. And the patients in the waiting room and corridors merely wondered if they would face the same fate if they had to wait much longer to be seen.

* * * * *

On Canvey Island, the whole unfortunate episode had had quite a profound effect. People were somewhat divided over it. On the one hand, Canvey was at last on the map - the coffee shop business was expanding rapidly as fans of TOWIE flocked to see the final resting place of Miss

Prissy. New jobs were created and a state-of-the art veterinary college was established. 'Fly on the Wall' was replaced by a new weekly programme broadcast from the centre, featuring the celebrity mega-vet, Stephen Spatchcock. Steven devoted 15 minutes of every programme exploring healthy treats for pets, in which local cats, accompanied by their servants, were invited in to sample the latest products on offer. Miss Prissy's servants were now redundant but had acquired minor celebrity status. Following a spate of interviews on daytime TV, they were able to finally afford leave their mobile home, and moved to the up and coming cockle sheds of Leigh-on-Sea.

One morning, the residents of Blenheim Place woke to find a major graffiti artist had decorated the lamp post under which Miss Prissy had finally met the Big Cat in the Sky. Dangling down from the lamp was a monumental aluminium wasp, whilst climbing up the post was an amazing array of multi-coloured, ceramic snakes. In the centre was a portrait of Miss Prissy, complete with her jewel-bedecked collar. And on the ground was an inscription which read, "Best wishes to my furry feline friend, from one Cool Cat to another. Signed: 'the artist formerly known as Banksy'.

Some people laughed, some people cried, and many of the TOWIE fans asked who the heck was Banksy? The reputation of Essex both rose a little and dropped a little that day, depending on your point of view. Angus Merryweather never worked in media again, and had an aversion to all animals and wildlife for the rest of his long life. He took up residence in one of the unoccupied beach huts along the seafront at Weston-Super-Mare. He felt quite at home there as there was a reassuring familiarity about the place, not dissimilar to Southend but with donkeys (which it has to be said he was quite ambivalent about). Still, the plus point was that the beach hut was situated a long way from the wretched donkeys, and Weston-Super-Mare was a long, long way from Essex. What Angus did not appreciate, however, was that 'the artist formerly known as Banksy' had a long and fascinating connection with Weston-Super-Mare, and had already ear-marked both Angus and the beach hut to be part of his next surprise exhibition.

But, for the time being, Angus remained blissfully unaware, lobbing the occasional stone at any seagulls that dared to come within ten feet of his castle. He eschewed anything to do with the media, possessing neither a television, mobile phone nor internet. He was therefore quite unaware that his little private hermitage was to be one day broadcast across the globe on Sky News. That was until the day he opened his wooden door to be confronted by Japanese tourists and the flash of a hundred camera lenses. Fame had found Angus once again, but that, dear readers, is another story.

Calumnied

by Sally Ann Nixon

Storm Callum was doing its worst, mugging the entire county of Carmarthen. The storm had howled all day. Flooding, landslides and wind to take you off your feet. The trees along the old twisted track bent and moaned in its wake. Branches snapped and cracked as the rain sluiced down, water rising in the yard, turning it into a sea of sodden leaves, twigs and unidentified floating objects. Plastic bags, rubbish from the fields and surrounding woods spun into the air and belly flopped down into my yard, trapped by the oaks and the gate. My friend had arrived somehow, risking death on the Merthyr Valley road, aquaplaning through the Beacons and finally splashing up the in semi darkness, under black cloud. Now we were drinking tea and we peered out at the storm. Opaque goblins shrieked in glee outside. Lights flickered on and off. Television and the internet had died hours ago, The boiler had blown out and the wood burner smoked. Things looked grim.

Tommy, the huge hound, needed a walk but there were no volunteers and besides, he was reluctant to go out in the gale. My old dog, Bella, Had more sense. She tiptoed over the gravel as quickly as she could, wincing at flying leaves and acorns. She did whatever she had to do and bumbled back in as fast as possible.

A crash!! That was the bin going over. We staggered out,

righted it and pushed it into a more sheltered spot. The door to the workshop had blown open and was flapping wildly. We tried to tie it up by the handle and hasp before it tore itself off. The cats watched impassively from the window ledge. Such struggles were beneath them and they felt that we should know better. We managed to tie the door tight and padlocked the gate before struggling against the gale, drenched and shivering.

A miracle! The power had come back on. It did not last long but at least we were able to boil the kettle, change our sopping clothes and fill hot water bottles to snuggle against the cold. It grew darker so we lit the candles we had stood ready. They danced precariously in the draught from the fireplace. Time passed, punctuated by brief returns of electricity, complaining cats, snoring dogs and our own quiet conversation. We read, talked and the daylight slipped away.

At 6 o'clock the power finally reconnected for good. We had light, a way of cooking properly and if I could just get the boiler to reignite, even heat through the house. I turned the cooker on low and a slow warmth filled the kitchen and the hall, whilst I fiddled with the boiler controls. Nothing worked. Oh well. Between hot drinks, the stoves and nice thick cardies we wouldn't freeze.

My son made it home through mud and flood and shut off roads. With no hope, I pointed to the boiler. He looked scathing, flipped up a panel on the boiler itself and pushed a big, red button. Abracadabra, it made a sort of boom and lit. One more hurdle cleared. Outside, the wind seemed to have calmed a little, though the rain still cascaded down. We fed the animals and started to heat up a casserole, whilst my son changed out of his work clothes and into his dog walking gear - waterproof everything and stout wellies.

Bella passed on it, pleading old age. Tommy, tail up, head down thrust his snout into the yard and sniffed - lots of interesting smells and noises but wet, wet, WET. Tommy wasn't sure about it but my so got behind and pushed and with much grumpling, Tommy slunk to the gate. We waved them goodbye through the storm, feeling a little as if we were waving to the Titanic. My son promised to be only half an hour. We promised the casserole would be ready on his return and asked him not to get blown off the mountain or down a bank into a ditch. Off they went, Tommy blundering, my son keeping his feet with the help of my Nordic poles, whilst the cats sneered from the windows.

We pottered around the kitchen, poured two glasses of wine and waited. The wind returned with a triumphant roar and the windows shook. The oaks threshed and sang a song of defiance as it grew darker still. We grew worried. This was not a night or a country to be out on your own especially when your only companion was the World's stupidest dog.

Up on the hill, the wind buffeted my son as he struggled to stay upright. Head well down, minding his step, he walked into the storm as it whooped around him. They had only a short way to go along the ridge but it was increasingly dark with no moon or stars to help and he didn't want to waste torch battery. The air was full of sounds, leaves bits of branch, mossy twigs and the rain blew into his wellies. Tommy was bothered. He had never seen anything like this in his short 18 months of life. He had spent his first and only winter in Southend, in a town and this wild land which he had romped through all summer was turning on him. The track, the ridge and the woods were home but had become strange. Nothing sounded or smelt as it should. My son turned on the torch as Tommy hunched against the tempest and for the woods in its faint glow. The wind made his body judder and his ears stream back. Tommy was aware of the watcher on the hill, quite close by but he ignored him as usual. No threat there. But ahead the small things in the trees were chattering and swinging around and around in excitement as the gusts grew stronger The wind veered around a little thumping Tommy's tail and the small ones in the wood clapped maliciously.

A great gust, wind sprite, storm ridden bore down on the hound. Deliberately, it crescendoed its shriek just behind him, then swooped skywards in an arabesque above the oaks.

Tommy spun round. Nothing. A great bang and a scream made by ... nothing! Acorns puttered down ahead of him and another shriek zoomed by him. Tommy had had enough. Loping low to the ground, neck stretched, ears flat to his head, he crashed through fern, bramble and bracken, through the woods, ignoring the reaching thorn bushes. He could hear the man calling and thudding flat footed after him but didn't stop. He could see the lights of home in the distance and he raced straight forward, down the path, up the track and over the gate. He rammed into the door with a howl. "I'm cold. I'm wet. I'm scared. Let me in!"

Mab put her head on one side and smiled superciliously from her perch in the porch. "Lost your man have you? Shame on you."

We heard Tommy howl and ran to the door. He was in a state, covered in drool and leaves, bleeding from scratches, wet through and shaking with cold and fright. My friend grabbed a towel and began to dry the dog, careful around his scrapped and bloody snout and paws. Where was my son? I tried to phone him but of course there was no signal. Had he been flattened by a falling bough, tripped, been blown over and hit his head? Telling myself not to be so dramatic, I pulled on my boots, took up my pole and started out of the door when the gate creaked.

" Is he back here?" A worried voice yelled above the din of the storm, which seemed to be concentrating itself right above my soaking yard, sending the leaves in a mad circle dance. From her perch, Mab watched the Thing Under the Wall raise his bones to conduct the crazed swirl.

" Such a show off." she hissed across the yard.

"As if they would take notice of the likes of you."

The Thing lifted his shoulder in a scornful shrug and twirled a beech wand like a baton.

My son, eyes and nose streaming, boots full of water,

stomped up the path.

" It's bad up there Mum. Tommy got scared, panicked and ran away. I followed him. We were just going along the Ridge when it came straight at us. We really felt like we were under attack."

"Oh you were, you were," sang the small ones turning windblown cartwheels in the oaks above.

"Just a game, don't complain, you're still alive!"

And with a scream of delight they skittered up the trees and away back to the wood.

The Watcher had seen it all before. Shepherds stumbling in search of their flock, sheep and cows scattering in fear with storm wraiths clinging to their tails, foxes and badgers waiting it out in their holes under the hill, squirrels clinging to their drays. Only mad men and their dogs go out in the storm.

Well, that was nice...

By Jayne Hecate

As a rational person I resolutely denied the existence of the supernatural, I was an adherent of Dawkins and as far as I could tell the stories of heaven and hell were simple stories used to instil values and morals in populations who lacked simple scientific knowledge. Or to put it indelicately as I often did, it was in my less than humble opinion, all a load of old bollocks. Which meant that when I ended up in the pit of hell, impaled upon the sharp end of a pitch fork, wielded by a red skinned, be-horned demon, as I waited for my first appointment with Satan; I was a little surprised to say the least.

Satan was actually rather charming, in the same way that a bank manager foreclosing on your home and all of your possessions is all sympathetic right up until they inform the bailiff to change the locks on the front door. Satan sat at her desk, her face a mixture of angelic beauty and gaunt prison guard. She was beautifully dressed, wearing a dark blue business suit of a knee length skirt and elegant jacket. Were it not for the curled horns coming from her perfectly combed hair, I would have thought her to be a tax inspector! Her blouse was a deep scarlet and made from the finest silk that shone in the lamp light. She stood up and crossed the rough rocky floor to a small water dispenser and poured herself a glass of ice cold fluid into a plastic disposable cup. She drained the cup and threw it into a pile that stood in the corner of a large cavern. She had clearly been doing this for millennia, the pile was the size of a large inner city hill. Occasionally there would be sudden screams from the damned when a landslide of cups swamped the dilapidated and filthy shanty they had built on the banks of the stagnant river.

Satan's heels click-clacked across the rocky floor as she took the slow steady steps back to her desk, refreshed. Pointing to a chair opposite her own, she asked me to sit down and cut the deck of cards that sat on the polished wooden surface. Given where we were, I was surprised that the desk had not suffered greater damage from the flames that seemed to lick up the sides of anything that remained still for more than a few minutes.

I cut the deck and placed the pack back on the desk in front of Satan, with a cool smile she took the pack and began to lay out a small diamond of cards. Most of them were pretty nondescript, describing how I had lived my life, where I had gone and all of the fairly minor sins I had committed. All of it was unremarkable, my whole life was pretty much wasted. I had done nothing that I truly enjoyed, produced offspring who grew up indifferent to me, as I was indifferent to them. My wife had spent the last years of our marriage involved in a shallow and unexciting affair with a woman from her tennis club. It was all so boring. My regrets were suddenly so big. My urge to travel had been crushed by apathy. My urge to paint buried by crap television. My only hobby of cataloguing toy cars, a mass of tiny cardboard boxes stored in a glass case was reduced pretty much to recording serial numbers in a computer spreadsheet. I was an accountant at home as well as at work. Satan looked up from her reading and gave me such a look of pity. She knew that it was too late, my life was gone.

The final card she played before me was significant. This was my future, this was the card that I had chosen with my splitting the deck. This single card was the rest of my existence. Some of the cards spoke of rebirth, some spoke of the end of suffering. Mine spoke of bondage and imprisonment. Satan sighed and seemed to sag slightly in seat. I am not sure if it was her sadness or mine that effected me the most. After clearing away the cards, she lifted the handset from an ancient turn dial phone and dialled a single number. After a few seconds the call was answered and I heard her one sided conversation. Some one called Harriet was to come down to Satan's office to collect me.

When Harriet arrived, she was a snot encrusted, porcupine quilled beast with three legs and the unendurable stench of raw human sewage emanating from her armpits. Her voice was gentle and she seemed rather kind as she asked me to accompany her to her place of work. As we made our way through the claustrophobic fumes and dark tunnels, she chatted merrily, asking me about my life, had I been happy, how did I feel about small spaces. Finally we reached a large, ancient door, carved from rough logs and banded together with sharp edged, corroded iron straps. She shoved the door open on its rusted hinges and showed me inside. As she closed the door, three large demons grabbed me from behind, bent me in two and crammed me into a tiny splinter covered wooden crate. The lid was fitted and then firmly nailed shut. A couple of the nails had split through the wooden sides of the crate and stuck painfully into my flesh, but I was barely able to draw breath, let alone move away from their sharp points.

With the crate nailed shut, I was lifted onto a sack truck and one of the demons began to push me into the darkness, having wished a cheery see you later to Harriet. So this is where I end my story, crammed into a tiny crate, left in the dark of a dripping cavern, the creeping insanity of it has crushed my desire for anything other than to stand up straight, even if just for a moment of relief.

Spring journey

By Margaret Ingram

The days at the centre flew by with timely highlights . Gretchen revelled in the learning. The formal classroom sessions were many but varied and the research to complete assignments was a joy. So many new things to understand that she didn't know that the weeks and months were passing. On top of that there were required activities as varied as any decadan could wish, from swimming in the centre's warm baths and sailing on the lakes around to swords and arbalests to master and even dancing many weekends. She tried to learn to play some of the many instruments available and finally found she was quite good at the claryn which had a sweet, mellow sound. She learnt a few tunes well enough to perform occasionally at parties, though she never really enjoyed the practice it took. She would have preferred to sing but 'couldn't carry a tune in a bucket' according to her friends, although her voice sounded OK from inside her head.

It came as a shock one vendri to have Vinn send her a message that he was returning to her home village on route for a neighbouring province. As it was her anniversary soon would she like to accompany him and spend a couple of fivdys with her family, to return with him after he had completed his meeting?

Spending time with her family was a mixed idea, sweet and sour at the same time. She took his note to the garden of MaistreTolwe's house and sat in the cool spring sunshine trying to make her mind up. Her longing to see her father and tell him all the wonders she had encountered was strong but she didn't want to meet most of the rest of the family. Uncle would be good and cousin Bern, the tree warden would probably be interesting, though Ma would disapprove of her talking to him. She would have all her new clothes to support her importance but knew Auntie and Granma would see them as showing off. Which, she realised with a small giggle, was exactly what they were; showing off how different I am, which is not a bad thing, she decided. But showing off was not worth it alone. She had almost decided to thank Vinn but decline when Maistre Tolwe wandered towards her and sat beside her in the sunshine. He pulled his cloak around him and said " colder for an old man like me but still cool for you, Gretchen."

'I'm comfortable, thank you, Maistre. I've lots of layers on and it is so good to sit in sunshine again. I've spent too much time in libraries.." she broke off, slightly startled. "I never thought I'd say that. How times change!"

"Yes, they do. And the journey you have made has been monumental, Gretchen. Have you made a decision about going with Vinn, visiting your family?"

"Not yet, really. I'm not really sure what to do. Both going and staying have bad sides and I'm not sure the good sides are good enough to sort it out. In fact, the offer has just caused a problem which I wouldn't have had, really. I was quite happy without thinking about going home. And that's one of the problems. It isn't my home any more. I left for good on my decad day. However something is pulling me, lots of little things, really. Most of them not very nice or sensible."

"Like showing them how far you have moved into a world they don't know?"

"Exactly! Petty snobbery is not going to make me happier and I expect I'll end up feeling very angry and sad. No need to do that to myself."

"True. You are too sensible to enjoy that kind of petty revenge. Would it make it easier if I asked you to do some errands for me while you are there? I need to get some feedback from the tree wardens and from one or two others, like the regional magister and you could be an excellent go-between."

"They wouldn't be very flattered to be talking to a little girl, Maistre."

" You wouldn't be the first youngster I've used and the previous ones have all justified my faith in their abilities. Vinn can introduce you to the local magister, Pahl Mikichan and Pahl can take up your introductions from there. He is a bright man and will probably welcome your father's daughter. Which is another reason to go, seeing your father and uncle should cheer you up."

"Do you think it would be acceptable to your contacts? And will you want me to talk to any of the local Maistres?"

"Well, definitely the tree wardens, especially Bern and his friends. They are a special little thread running through the tree wardens who keep an eye on special people like you. I'd like you to learn more about them. Apart from that your region possesses some of the most inept Maistres in the land. We keep them there for ease of control. They have a good life and we can watch their little plots to ensure they don't get big and ugly. That's one of the reasons people like your Grandparents fit in so well. It can make it hard for you and other interesting individuals but we can usually give some protection, like we did for you."

"Me?"

"Didn't you ever wonder why your father and uncle got so many visitors? Noone else was seeing outsiders so regularly, even the inn, and we made sure you lived on a through-route for trade.

Your father's habit of offering lodging to tinkers and tradesmen was a way of opening up your little world. It's working for your young brother, Crill, too. He'll follow you to a centre, on his decad."

"A centre? Is there more than one?"

"There are two more, one for mechanics and engineers and one for .. well for people who serve and protect society. That one is part of the Ministry. I think Crill will be an engineer who has crazy ideas which he makes work. He is a bit young to be sure yet, but he may come here also. No one in your family will be going into the third centre. You lot are too honest for that. However, that is a side road and we need to get you sorted. I would like you to go home with Vinn to allow me to use you as liaison with some of my eyes and ears. I also feel it would be good for you to establish in your family that you are working and should be deferred to by ordinary people. I think you can keep your work on an understated level which will seriously annoy your mother and aunt."

Gretchen grinned. "I like the sound of that. And it will be good to have the authority to behave as an adult, making decisions and being purposeful and not having to hang around the family. It will please Pa to see me again and I can hardly wait to see him. When is Vinn leaving, do you know? I need to buy some presents if I am going."

"You have about 10 days. I'll need to instruct you on your missions but you should be able to shop around. I think we can offer you a pack mule since I want you to bring back some reports and samples and things. You had better let Vinn know, ask for dates and let me know after lunch so we can set up some training sessions for you. That gives you about two hours to plan your present list."

She bounced up, curtsied with a mumbled 'thank you' and sped off to her room to get the acceptance note written and sent and to start listing presents and checking her finances. Half way there she suddenly thought she should have asked Tolwe whether he would pay her for the trip? That would be the cherry on the cake, to visit them and to be on official business, getting paid for her time! ;After lunch,' she thought,' I can ask after lunch.'

Spike

By Geraldine Paige

Watching a film about motorcycles dating from 1930 to 1950. I remembered that I had a bike about the same age in my garage waiting to be rewired . Next morning, thinking to myself that it was about time I started work on my bike I went out to my garage. I knew that sometime back I had bought electrical cable especially for the job. So, in theory it should not have taken me long to get everything together that I needed to finish the job.

WRONG . Could not find the electrical cable. Seeing that the cable in question was really 8 individual cables, each one covered in different colours plastic, and about 1 metre in length. I should have been able to put my hands on it in on time at all. Some days later, I came to the conclusion that I must have been mistaken, and had not bought the cable after all.
Looking through my Motor Bike Magazine for the date of the next Auto-jumble where I could buy some more cable for my bike, a piece of paper fell out and landed on the floor. When I picked it up, I realized that I had bought the cable after all, here was the receipt. Well, one problem solved. I was not losing my mind. But where on Earth was the cable? . After the Auto-jumble and with my nice new cable in my hot little hand , I started work on my bike.

About a fortnight later I was congratulating myself on a job well done. However, while working in the Garage there was one thing that I had found a little bit unusual . I was aware that on occasions there had been a very strange rasping noise in the garage. No, it was not someone's radio. I was determined to find out where the noise was coming from. So one afternoon I just sat and listened in the garage. It was coming from under a bench that was situated in one of the corners . I managed to move the heavy bench enough for me to get around to the back. All I found was a pile of oily rags that somehow must have fallen down. Went to pick them `OUCH`. I immediately dropped the rags. Something had hurt my hand. After giving my hands a good wash in hot soapy and disinfected water, I put a pair of gloves on and went back to the pile of oily rags. With my hands now protected, not only did I manage to pick up the rags, I was now able to put them onto the bench. Then I set about unravelling the rags. Low and behold there was my electrical cable followed by some of my nice shiny spanners which had also vanished into thin air. But that was not all I had found inside that pile of oily rags. What had hurt my hand? How did the cable and spanners get there?

It was a very large Hedgehog, a sleeping, very large Hedgehog. I had now met Spike. I gently wrapped him back up in his oily rags and my tools, then put him back where I had found him. Went into my home and made a cup of tea. We became inseparable, there were three people in our marriage. Late evenings I had to leave the garage door open so that Spike could forage in the garden for food. But I had to make sure that Spike was back safe and sound in the mornings, so I could shut the garage door if I was going out for the day. This went on for sometime, and we got to know each other very well, because if for some reason I had to shut the garage door and was a bit late in getting back, he would be sitting there waiting for me.

One day Spike decided that he would change his address, he moved from behind the bench to a cupboard. On doing so, he left the cable, spanners and oily rags behind. I was so pleased to have my things back, I made him a nice new nest with clean rags and paper as a house warming present. I must say that the sound of Spikes gentle snoring during the day while I was working, had a very soothing effect. Some months later, this friendship came to an end the night Spike went out for his nightly forage and never came back. So readers. If you hear a gentle snoring sound, and you have lost some cable and spanners, and it turns out to be Spike. Can you please send him home. I miss him. Thank you.

One last smile

by Stephen Breakspear

To Sammy it was a simple no-brainer about what got him up each day. His chosen reason for living was to make twelve people that he met each day smile, and in a city like New York that wasn't easy. Twelve people because he was twelve this year, and, for the duration of that birthday year it was always going to be twelve people; twelve years old, twelve smiles; thirteen years old, thirteen smiles, a no-brainer. Every so often he became concerned about getting older and not achieving his increasing target, but now was not the time to worry about that. To Sammy it was a simple, self-evident reason that was clear to him should the need ever arise to explain his motivation; but nobody ever asked him; anything; ever. Very few people noticed Sammy except for twelve people each day, including weekends.

Sammy's concern was that he wasn't sure he was twelve but, in the scheme of things, Sammy didn't see that as a stumbling block. Sammy had ground rules of course, that he had worked out for himself, and stuck to, rigidly. There had to be order to his system, or it would be worthless if rules were bent just to make it easier for himself. Sammy didn't count children as they usually smiled when they saw him anyway, too easy.

Smiles had to be genuine; a simple polite smile didn't count, especially if it wasn't full face. Sammy had frequently considered as he got older, and his daily count increased annually, it would be fair to count full blown laughter as maybe a double smile, easing his work. But Sammy felt; knew; deep down, that this was cheating and cheating didn't really appeal to him if his work was to mean something.

He considered allowing himself to carry over additional smiles above his quota from day to day but again felt that it would be bad form to bend, or break, his own rules. For that reason he had set his days to run from midnight to midnight, not a minute more, and not a minute less.

This was why he was still out on the streets at 11:30 pm on that very cold November night, all because of his midnight rule. Pickings had been slim today, people were hurrying about because of the cold, and the dark had come early leaving Sammy short by one smile with only a half hour to go.

There was no-one about and it was starting to snow again and time was very, very short to make up his daily smile count of twelve. Sammy had always got twelve smiles each day since his 'assumed' birthday twelve months ago. He didn't want to fail now, not by just one smile. Sammy prided himself on going that extra mile, making that last effort to succeed.

Sammy passed from intersection to intersection through the whitened, muffled streets daubed with lonely pools of yellow light. As he reached each crossroad he stopped to look into the distance in four directions hoping for his final chance of that night. As he changed streets and direction each time he could hear all sorts of carols and Christmas music in the distance. Although different they all seamlessly blended together to colour the Christmas card look of the whitened, empty streets.

Then, with only about 15 minutes to go he caught sight of three people standing still in a small group in the shadows between the street lights. Three chances, one smile, good odds.

Sammy ran toward them as best he could through the deepening snow, slipping and sliding every so often, but recovering each time. It was hard work with time going on and a small seed of desperation, the start of panic, growing inside Sammy as he closed on the group.

In the gloom between the street lights, and random splashes of light from naked windows, he could make out the dark silhouettes of the three men silently facing each other, standing like statues with the distant sound of Christmas all around them.

At twenty feet away he could see that one man had his back to him, Sammy knew that people often don't like to be surprised, especially if you want to make them smile, and so he barked out a greeting to them.

The two men facing in his direction looked up, and noticed him for the first time. From 15 feet away he could see the surprise on their faces illuminated by the weak reflected light from the quietly falling snow. The man with his back to him stiffened as he noticed their attention was diverted over his shoulder. As he turned he was still a dark outline but Sammy saw that he seemed to hold a bright shining star that lived for the briefest of instants, just as Sammy felt the thump at his chest that slowed him to a crawl, and long before he heard the noise of the gun that killed him.

Taking their opportunity the two men grabbed the mugger and dragged him to the ground, face down, taking his gun and pinning him down. The larger of the two men knelt on his back and shouted to his friend, "Help him, I've got this one, he ain't gonna move. Now go!"

Sammy lay slumped in the snow and watched wearily as the white snow changed to red around him. Sammy saw the two men down in the snow and the third run toward him shouting. Sammy saw the man's mouth move but couldn't hear the words. Sammy noticed that the street lights were growing dimmer. Sammy felt warm and comfortable, the best he had ever felt in his miserable life, he didn't even feel hungry any more.

The man was bending over him now, looking with caring, worried eyes and he gently stroked Sammy's fur and muzzle. Sammy saw him mouth one more thing and it looked like "Thank you", but for what, Sammy didn't know.

Then the man smiled.

One for the Toad

By Sally Ann Nixon

" No, its not a phallic symbol".

Mrs Pritchard was nearly in tears of frustration and annoyance.

Jim Satterthwaite looked sceptical and played his last card.

"And its not a Welsh thing. We don't want no foreign imports at the carnival."

Mr Satterthwaite, despite his Yorkshire origins was a dedicated Welshman .Sandra tried to inject a little common sense.

"Its true that its an English thing but so is the idea of a carnival in the first place. And I don't know what the origins of the maypole are. Celtic, I think. But I'm sure that everyone will see it for what it is - a charming dance to spring."

"Bloody fertility rite. Minister don't like it."

"Mr Satterthwaite!!"

"What is wrong with a dance to welcome the Spring, performed by the pupils at Yglys.."

"Well, I'm against it. What's wrong with a nice clean egg and spoon?"

"That Welsh is it? Long handles on the spoons. Eggs at the end. What can your grubby mind make of that,Mr Satterthwaite?"

Mrs Pritchard was determined to have the last word.

"If you are going to be offensive..."

Mr Satterthwaite stamped his wellies and stomped across the station car park to the Lord Rhys.

" Bloody airey fairy lot. Bloody maypole. Be fancy dancey morris men next."

He slammed the door into the pub after him, Leaving the remainder of the carnival committee on the pavement outside the station cafe. They watched him go. The last male committee member seemed to have resigned. Sandra's husband was prepared to help set up and Mr Pritchard was happy to transport things in the horse box but the actual organisation they left to their wives. John Satterthwaite had voted with his feet. Declared defeat. Pulled out. Withdrawn, in fact.

"Nice bit of man management , that, Heffina."

They filed into the cafe, hired as their planning room for the day and locked the door. Heffina Pritchard patted her tight perm and straightened the tablecloth on the refectory table whilst Hara pulled down the blinds. Sandra fished a statuette of the Goddess out of her deep, knitted tote bag and placed it on the north facing table, overlooking the railway line. Somehow the little cafe had a sacred space amongst the tea cups, the women were there to the power of three and the moon was waxing that night.

"An auspicious time." said Heffina Pritchard.

She invoked the Guardians and at each quiet call, the women turned widdershins. They dedicated the carnival to the Goddess, commended the dance and Spring song to her care and invoked her benign influence to spread over the town.

In the Lord Rhys, Mr Satterthwaite shivered and stamped again.

"Eee. Someone just walked over my grave."

He glanced towards the shuttered cafe.

"Bloody women."

The Sale

By Margaret Ingram

In 1941, after the defeat of France by the Nazi forces, France was divided into 3. Northern France was ruled by a German occupying regime, most of the rest of France was ruled by the collaborationist Vichy government led by Petain, but a small slice of south-eastern France, the old Savoie, along the Mediterranean coast, was ruled by Mussolini's Fascists. Nice was the main city in this area and became a very unsafe magnet for some Jews and Blacks who tried to escape from there to Switzerland or by sea to North Africa.

Josie was almost dancing with impatience. "Come on Liz, it's a chance to get some wonderful bargains. I got a sable jacket for 1500 francs! Real sable. For the price of a good dinner! You just can't believe the prices. I know the stuff is all used but such stuff. Haute couture, silk and satin and we're doing them a favour, they'd starve without the money."

Josie sucked in a great big breath after delivering this, which gave Liz a chance to speak. That's how you had to work it with Josie. She spoke in a continuous stream until her breath ran out.

"Why don't they just go somewhere where they can live a normal life?"

"They can't, silly. They are on waiting lists to go to USA or Argentina and so on but no one wants them. There are quotas and, I was talking to one of them a few weeks ago and she said she had a visa coming up in two months but had to live until then and find her fare and couldn't take all the things with her so she was desperate to sell anything she could. I mean, don't get me wrong, you could buy anything there, furniture, cars, anything. I even saw houses for sale, they have a picture and a description and you arrange to go see it. M B, you know, the lighting engineer, he got a lovely coupe like that and he is always getting wonderful clothes here. Mind you he is short and fat! So he is the right shape," she giggled, "to get Jew-boys' clothes that fit."

'That's awful, Josie. You sound like that administrator in Props. He's a real Nazi, always going on about the German films and making nasty comments about communists and Jews."

"You mean that slimy thin type with the Douglas Fairbanks moustache, he wishes? It looks like a cat sicked up a furball on his top lip. I've never seen anyone else with curly hair in his moustache."

This set them giggling like a pair of schoolgirls but they quietened down in the stairwell of Liz's apartment. It didn't do in this time to annoy the concierge or to get a reputation for rowdy behaviour unless it was with State officials, soldiers, sailors or Nazi visitors. Concierges could denounce you and, although Liz thought she got on well with Mme. Clirot, she was not taking any chances. Of course, good behaviour didn't guarantee safety but she relied on the French habit of 'wait and see' to work on her side in the equation. If she gave little offence she would probably be safe.

The sunshine in the street made them straighten up and the two women set off for the sale arm in arm with Josie still talking. If you didn't know them you would not realise that her topics had become totally banal once she was in the street. Liz listened and was amazed that anyone could talk so much about nothing. She knew Josie did it to make herself more noticeable and more noticed. She was nineteen and determined to be a big movie star although her acting ability was limited. She had told Liz that she knew she was not a great actress, but she also knew the camera loved her and she was very attractive in a faintly predatory, blousey way. In previous centuries she would have aimed at being a high level courtesan, perhaps, or of getting a wealthy husband if she was lucky. In these modern times she was making her play for fame and wealth in celluloid. Liz thought Josie would make it if she had even average luck. The right moment to be noticed by an important director or producer, a small part successfully completed and then bigger parts or a jump to a big chance, Josie would take each step and use her chance. Liz knew Josie was walking a tightrope but if anyone could get across to the other side Liz would put her money on Josie.

The girls kept linked arms as they walked through the town, heading inland along steadily widening streets as they moved further from the promenade and climbing the ascending pavements as they went into the hills that led towards the gorges and Alps behind Nice. They finally climbed an alleyway of broad steps which led up to the old Roman settlement, where most of the buildings were Maisons Bourgeois and 19th century Hotels.

These roads were lined with trees and the area was very quiet, which made the car sitting outside the gates of the maison they turned into so much more noticeable.

Josie ignored the car but Liz turned and looked in as they passed it. Inside there were three middle-aged men who looked like police for some reason Liz couldn't put her finger on. They watched the women with deadpan faces. One turned away as she watched and looked at a man walking past on the other side of the road. The man kept his eyes down except for one quick glance at the car. He walked faster after the glance. Liz turned to Josie.

"What do you think those men are looking at?"

"Jews, I suppose. They don't seem interested in people like us. They're always there when I come to these sales. They are the French Milice so they have no power here since the Italians took over, Grace Dieu."

"Aren't you worried? Suppose they got nasty about mixing with Jews. You know the general order forbids employing them."

"I think they quite like the idea that we are stripping the Jews of their stuff for peanuts. You sometimes see the police talking to buyers but they seem to be friendly and I saw them giving one woman a ride back to town with her purchases. She was thanking the one in the front for his kindness so I know she wasn't being arrested. I wonder if I asked them .."

"Don't you dare, Josie!"

Josie laughed, "Calm down, silly. The fare would be too high for a nice Catholic girl like me."

They had walked to the front of the Maison and now Josie went around to the side and then to a small door in the back wall. She led Liz in and along a dark corridor. They went up a winding stair and through another door into a marble floored hall. Josie stopped and looked around. "Isn't it beautiful? When I'm rich I want a house like this." She walked slowly out into the centre of the hall and then seemed to shake herself. "Over there," she pointed to their left and walked towards a door, which was ajar. They walked into a large room full of very quiet people among tables covered with clothes and goods. It was like an indoor flea market without the vivacity and colour. Liz felt her skin crawling. There was something horrible about the desperation she felt in that room. Josie seemed totally unaware of it, but that might be because this was not the first sale she had been to. Perhaps it seemed more normal after a few visits.

The room was magnificent in proportion, with a high ceiling and big windows on two sides but rather in need of redecoration. The paint work showed where pictures or mirrors had been removed and there were scuff marks and scratches . Gilt touches were tarnished or flaky in places and the light fittings had been removed. The windows were dirty and there were no drapes or curtains.

Packed into this space were six rows of tables with narrow walkways between them. People, obviously the owners of the goods piled on the table, were standing behind each table. These were men and women in good clothes but with an air of tension, some smoking too much, lighting one cigarette from another, shifting nervously, one chewing her nails, another winding her hair around her finger then unwinding it as though it was her clockwork to keep her going.

A thin stream of buyers walked slowly around, reaching for goods, picking them up and examining them, sometimes talking to the sellers, putting things back more often than they bought. They were quiet and had an air of disapproval on their faces, hoping to get cheaper prices by hiding their interest in any item. The buyers were not as well dressed as the sellers and one or two looked very down-at-heel. One Liz recognised as having a shop which sold second-hand clothes in the old town. She thought the clothes here were too good for that shop but the woman was buying a few items and stuffing them into a big bag slung over her shoulder. She haggled for each piece as though she was destitute but had a big purse with her. Liz watched her a couple of times as she made her way round the room.

Josie led Liz to their right and started to walk through the room. Josie was quiet for a change, looked at the goods for sale and sorted out the items she wanted to examine more closely. She said nothing now and bought nothing, walking slowly. Liz looked at the goods on the tables but also looked at the people.

They finished their journey around the room, a stately circumnavigation to identify the best items to buy. Liz had seen a pair of evening shoes and an evening dress, which she thought she might buy for the next studio party. She'd worn the same dress three times now and the parties were important for extras like her to keep in the eye of the casting people. Given the type of pictures that were being made at the moment she needed to have a bit of glamour about her.

In a quiet voice Josie said, "Did you see anything? I'm going for that blue dress and bag over there," and pointed to the far side of the room. "If I can get that cheap enough I'll try for that silk frock we saw as we came in, the one with the poppies on it. What about you, did you see anything?"

"Soon after we came in, that black and green evening dress and the shoes she had there too. I saw a shirt for Jean-louis, too, just there, in the middle. Are you going to try for that suit for Emile? You looked like you were very interested. "

"No, I was more interested in the shoes with it but they will be too narrow for Emile. Shall we split up? Or do you want to work together?"

"Let's split up. I need to be back by 5 and its getting late." Truth be told she wanted to be away from Josie's predatory air. She felt like a rat, too aware of how desperate the sellers were to enjoy the prices and the goods. She wanted to offer the asking price, which was cheap enough , and not haggle. She had enough for the dress and shoes and for the shirt without bargaining. That way she would be able to wear the things with a good conscience. They went their separate ways and Liz went straight for the dress and shoes. She checked them over and got out her money. The women who was selling gaped at her for a moment then shut her mouth and took the money. As Liz picked up the dress and shoes the woman offered her a bag which obviously matched the shoes. "No," said Liz, "I can't .."

"Free for you, M'am'selle , for not haggling. I asked more than I would get so take this free." And she pushed the bag into Liz's hand. Their eyes met and the woman smiled. "I have no use for the bag any more and if I get to South America I will buy new. You will look good in the dress."

"Thank you." Liz said and turned away quickly. She walked towards the stall with the shirt but felt a hand on her arm. It was a little woman with a basket of make-up.

"Please, pretty girl, you need make-up to go with the dress. Please buy." She tried to smile but her face was a grimace and her eyes were terrified. Liz nearly recoiled then started to fish around in the basket. She found a lipstick with a good colour and most left and asked how much. "a hundred, pretty lady. It will suit you so much."

Liz knew if she bought this she would have to bargain for the shirt or not buy it. She started to decline but the Josie came up. "Oh yes Liz, buy it. It is perfect for you and that dress." The old woman's eyes lit up and she pushed the lipstick at Liz. Liz took out the money and gave it to the old woman. Josie rummaged through the basket and found some lipstick and skin cream to buy.

They turned away and walked on. "Why," asked Liz, "didn't you argue about the price?"

113

"She keeps her husband and a disabled son on what she can get at these sales. She has sold almost everything and now she sells her old cosmetics. I've seen her peddling them around the Marche Aux Fleurs and one of the waiters in a bar told me. He had given her a drink. He said she had been his school teacher when he was younger and she had given his mother some chicken soup every week while his father was out of work. He said that soup was the only good meal the family had each week for a couple of months. He said that his birthday had fallen during that time and the teacher had made him a cake which had given the whole family food for a week. Mind you, he had said, he still couldn't eat fruit cake to this day, he had got so sick of it. So I always buy something from her." Josie had told this quietly and gravely, not in her normal vivacious style. Then her head came up and she said, "This shirt, where was it?"

"It doesn't matter now." said Liz. "I can't afford it now."

"Nonsense, I'll sub you and we can settle up later." And Josie led the way until they found the shirt.

Back in the sunshine they walked up the drive and past the car. It was either a different car or the men had changed, Liz wasn't sure. She wanted to run away but she kept walking steadily past them and turned down the alleyway towards the town. From the top of the alleyway they could see a tiny arc of town and distant blue Mediterranean.

"Look at that," said Liz, "Can you think of anywhere more beautiful and yet we have just been involved in something so sordid."

Josie grasped her arm and gave it a little cuddle. "Don't think too hard, Liz, just do what good you can. And enjoy yourself when you can. At least you can stop getting Jean-Louis to paint your lips for a while." She looked deep into Liz's eyes and then laughed. "Listen to me! I sound like Garbo in one of her roles. Come on, Liz, let's get back to the real world." And she skipped down the steps pulling Liz with her until, laughing, they ran out of the end of the alley and into the broader street.

They walked back to Liz's home and parted. Liz asked Josie to come in for a drink but Josie had to get changed for a dinner engagement with a writer from the Studio. "He has suggested me for a couple of small parts and I want to keep him friendly. He doesn't ask too much, just a kiss and cuddle. I think his wife lets him do the deed but doesn't allow any romance or feeling. Weird world we live in. I'd sooner have the cuddles, not that I've ever done the deed, being a good catholic girl." And she looked at Liz and they both laughed, though Liz had an impression that Josie was being truthful. As she climbed the stairs to her apartment she thought about it. Josie wasn't naïve but there was some sort of freshness in her manner that suggested she didn't sleep around. Liz could believe that Josie could turn a man down without upsetting him, making it a joke and a secret between them. Josie was a consummate actress in real life and today's outing had made Liz more aware of this side of her friend's character than ever before.

Suddenly alone, she felt drained and walked slowly up to the apartment. She was just getting her key out when Jean-Louis opened the door. "My darling, how I have missed you!" he said in his most melodramatic voice and, gathering her up in his arms carried her and her bags into the sitting room, laughing. As they went through the door she saw two of his friends, Tonio and Jacques sitting on the couch. They were smiling and sipping small glasses of what looked and smelt like whiskey.

"See," said Jean-louis, "I told you I could feel her presence!" he put her gently down in the big armchair by the window and knelt beside her. "How can I win the favour of my darling princess?"

"Sweet Prince, just cease your play-acting and give me a drink." She said, making them all laugh.

Tonio poured a glass of the spirit and passed it to Jean-Louis who, in turn passed it to Liz. "Drink, my beloved, of the nectar of the gods."

She sipped and then said, in a Jean Harlow accent "Wow, big boy, this is the real McCoy. You sure know how to give a girl a good time."

"Enough, Liz." Said Jacques, "you are too much." and he clapped his hands in a parody of applause. Jacques hated to be upstaged by anyone. "So" she said, "where in all of the heavens you visit, my brave Jacques, did you get real Whisky?"

"Yes, now that Liz is back you have no excuse for not telling us." said Jean-Louis. "He wouldn't tell us until you got here, Liz even though I offered a kiss for the tale."

"What use do I have for your kisses," said Jacques, "When I have the love of a good man and you have the love of a good woman?"

"Enough, Jacques. Tell us do." Tonio turned to Jean-Louis and Liz. "I don't know what this is all about any more than you do. He has been so mysterious, the old queen."

Jacques looked about to start arguing with Tonio about this soubriquet, but then thought better of it. Perhaps, thought Liz, his innate sense of timing was going to save them from another delay.

"Well, mes amis, This morning I got a call from the studio and who do you think it was? No, don't even try to guess, you'll never be able to, so I'll tell you. I got a call at 10 a.m., 10 in the morning if you don't mind, what kind of time is that for a civilised call? Well, it isn't civilised is it? So I answered with my most suave 'qua?' and coughed down the phone just for good measure."

"Who was it?" screeched Tonio. "if you don't get on with it, I swear I'll strangle you, with my own hands."

"It was, well it was his secretary first, thank the good God, Can you imagine if it had been him I was rude to. Oh, I feel faint at the thought of it. My life would..."

Tonio grabbed Jacques neck in both hands and yelled "Who? Tell us now or I swear I will kill you and blame it on the Mistral."

"The Mistral isn't blowing." said Liz

"Who cares?" said Tonio. "I would be happy to die for this, this ..."

"All right, all right," said Jacques "it was Clouzot!"

They all stared at him.

"Hah! That has shut you all up. Henri-Georges Clouzot himself."

The silence stretched and they all waited with bated breath for him to go on. When Liz was about to ask, Jean-Louis beat her to it,

"Well, don;t stop there. What did he want? And don't pretend he just called to ask you for a dance at the next Carnival."

"He wanted me to write for his new film! Oh, not the script itself, he already has that, but any rewrites and so on. He wants me to sit around and fiddle with his script!"

"But," said Liz, jumping up, "That's wonderful."

"How much is he paying?" said Jean-Louis.

"Enough each week for me to live on and live well. This will let me write my book and get paid. So I bought the Whisky from a little old man I know who delivers to the American embassy and

117

came here to tell my very best friends. I have been saved, at least temporarily, from a life of penury and strife by the wonderful, the genius Clouzot! Long live Clouzot! He shouted and stood with his glass raised. They all jumped up and shouted "long live Clouzot" and then all 4 drank. Jean-Louis was quick enough to grab Jacques' glass from his hand before he threw it into the fireplace. "What is the film called?" he said to take Jacques mind back to the news.

"He called it The Raven. I couldn't care less what it's called. Regular money for being on hand to do a bit of writing now and then. Heaven!"

"This is something to celebrate," said Tonio, "let's get drunk."

"No," said Liz, I just bought a new evening dress and i want to show it off with three handsome men to escort me. Let's dine!"

"OK" said Jean- Louis, "and as the only one of the three men with any money Jacques can pay."

"Where is the nearest soup kitchen?" laughed Jacques, "but yes, lets dine. Tonio will pay this time and when Liz gets her star role at my recommendation, you can pay, J-L!"

They all laughed and agreed to meet in the Place Garibaldi at 7. Tonio and Jacques took the rest of their bottle and went home to change "in honour of Liz's new dress."

Jasper

By Jayne Hecate

Jasper was still a kitten when he turned up in my life, as bright and clever as you would expect a street smart cat to be, but there was something else about him, something that seemed to understand more about the world than you would have imagined. I was a science teacher at the time and was not what you would call in the market for another pet, having had to have my last cat put to sleep due to pneumonia, which broke my heart. So having this delightful little creature arrive in my home was in truth a little unwanted, but there was no getting rid of him. He adopted me and as such I became his human, rather than him becoming my cat. Even now, after twelve years of living together, Jasper still treats me like his pet human, although he has started to show his age now and has slowed down a little.

The first real inkling I got that he was a little brighter than most other cats in our area was when I came home from work and found that the cat treat box was completely empty, however the lid was still in place and there were no holes in the box. Jasper was fast asleep on the bed, his tummy swollen with dried cat treats. The only clue to the culprit of the theft was a tiny mark on the edge of the box that was the exact size of one of his claws. When I lay down on the bed that night, Jasper groaned and slowly climbed from the duvet to wander down stairs and out through the cat flap. When he returned several hours later, he was considerably less bulky and a lot more lively.

Now how he turned up in my house is a story in itself, you see a friend of mine awoke on the mornings after that terrific meteor shower, the one that really lit up the sky. As she was wandering around her kitchen, she put the children's cereal bowls on the side, ready to pour in the kids version of kibble and when she turned back, there was a ginger kitten sat on her work top. Slightly startled, she stared at him as he in turned stared at her. He looked no more than six weeks old, his eyes were still that funny colour they are before cats reach maturity. After a few seconds of silent staring, he meowed at her and she stroked his head, which he seemed to like. However, she lived in a block of flats and the rules were strictly no pets! After asking around if anyone had lost a kitten, for a few days and with feeding the foundling kitten, she needed to re-home him or find a new home for herself, the kids and him all together. Sadly, such a family move was not going to happen, so Jasper needed a place to stay for a few days until a new home could be found. Which is how he ended up at my Mother's. I popped in to visit her and Jasper jumped into my lap and refused to let go. When it came time for me to go home, we had to untangle his claws from my work jacket and as I left, he started to yowl so loudly, I could hear him as I walked back to my car.

For three days, Jasper refused to eat, drink or stop yowling. I popped in to see how Mum was doing and Jasper jumped into my lap, climbed up my chest and stared really hard into my face, swapping from each of my eyes to make sure that I got the message. When I stood up to leave, he wrapped himself around my neck and refused to let go. My mother trying to release him caused hissing and spitting and a nasty scratch to my Mother's hand. Thus I ended up with a cat.

The drive home was interesting, for a start, I had a ginger kitten wrapped around my throat, purring so loudly, I could barely hear the engine of my old Nissan Micra. At traffic lights, the drivers of other cars would pull up next to me and then notice Jasper. I got hard stares, people pointing and laughing and one very concerned look from a Policeman who just happened to be going another way. Thankfully, I managed to get home before I was stopped. As soon as I was in my place, Jasper uncurled from my throat and dashed up stairs where he hid under my bed for twenty minutes as I sorted out a couple of old cheap plastic cat bowls for him and a littler tray. Mum had given me a small bag of kibble for him, which I poured into one of the bowls and I filled the other with fresh tap water. As for the litter tray, I used an old baking tray that I lined with newspaper, thinking that I could always pick up some proper cat litter the next day when I came home from work.

My dinner that night was a microwave curry with rice and a naan bread. Jasper sat on the arm of my chair watching intently as I ate. His eyes followed my fork from the plastic bowl to my mouth and then back to the bowl. With out thinking, I offered him a piece of the chicken, but not really expecting him to take it, given the hot spices. He took the lump of chicken and placed it delicately on the arm of my chair and turned his eye to my spoon that I had been using for the rice. His stare was so intent that I actually found myself giving him a spoonful of rice too. He placed the lump of chicken on the rice, pushed it around until all of the soft warm grains were stuck to the meat and then he ate it. Once he had finished, sat up and began to wash his paws.

I finished my dinner and took my dishes out to the kitchen, where I could rinse the plastic bowl for the recycling and drop my cutlery into the holder for the dishwasher. Jasper's food bowls were untouched, he wandered across the floor to them and sniffed them disdainfully. When he sat down, he fixed me once again with a hard stare and I found myself wilting and quickly picked up the bowls. His gaze turned to the stack of antique bowls I kept on the shelf above the fridge and his meow sounded awfully like he was requesting one. I pointed at the bone china bowl and he rubbed his head against my ankle. So I then pointed at the plastic cat bowl and I swear that he gave me the most contemptuous look I have ever received. With the message clear, I filled the antique bone china bowl with water and took another into which I poured the cat kibble. I placed both bowls on the kitchen floor in front of the washing machine and again I was given a hard look of disapproval. I quickly picked them up and Jasper dashed from the kitchen, stopping at the door to meow until I followed him, the two bowls still in my hands. He led me through the house as he checked each room, before he finally settled on my office...

I signed Jasper up with a very good local vet and bought a new cat carrier so that I could take him for his first check up and to have him fitted with a microchip. I placed the carrier on my bed because he was fast asleep on my pillow, or so I thought, he opened one yellow eye and glared at the cat carrier with contempt, before returning to sleep. Suddenly worried for my well being, I got a thick bath towel and putting on my gardening gloves prepared to wake Jasper and place him into the cat carrier. He was fast asleep and lifting him was like trying to lift a jelly filled carrier bag, he seemed to flow through my fingers and I was concerned that he would turn into a liquid! But he just snored more loudly and continued to sleep. I got him in the box with the grace of a builder pouring cement into a wheel barrow. I closed the door of the box and Jasper remained fast asleep, he barely moved as I walked out of the house and put the box on the back seat of my car and he continued snoring as I started the engine and drove away.

However things changed very quickly as I entered the vets. I was signing him in for his check up, I had looked at him only seconds before and he had still been fast asleep, the nurse was very friendly and then suddenly she yelled out. Jasper's case simply fell apart. The plastic clips and metal screws that held it all together appeared to have all come loose at the same time. The bottom of the carrier and the metal wire door all fell to the floor. Jasper with the grace of an acrobat leapt from the collapsing box and landed on the door handle, which with his weight, slowly began to turn until the door swung open. Again with a speed that I found almost unbelievable, Jasper shot out of the door and into the busy street outside.

Luckily for me, the vets was built at the back of a very large and busy car park. As the door began to swing closed again, both the Nurse and I pelted through it and began to chase Jasper across the car park. With his small size and tremendous speed, he was able to dodge moving cars, run under parked cars and finally took shelter under the exact centre of a large builders van that was covered with cement dust and ladders. I was still wearing my grey skirt and jacket from school and with an indelicate action managed to slide on my back under the van, my legs coming out from under the side of the van. I grabbed Jasper's collar and wriggled my way back out from under the van, much to the amusement of the three jolly builders who were returning to the vehicle with arms full of plumbing supplies. Jasper crouched in my arms, his angry growling and furious eyes was enough to prevent the builders from stroking him, but one of them did give me a card with his phone number on it.

I looked down at my skirt and jacket, the skirt was fine, but I had managed to put my elbow in a large sticky oil drip on the tarmac under the van and the jacket was ruined. I also had a dirty face, my hair was messed up and the Nurse who had watched my crawl walked back to the vets with me, while trying to suppress her laughter. While Jasper was being checked over and given his chip, I bought a sturdy wicker basket for him. It had no plastic clips, no points that came apart for easy cleaning and best of all, an old fashioned strap and buckle closure system. The vet nurse kindle agreed to dispose of the plastic wreckage of my first one for me.

Over the summer holidays that year, the builder from the van whose name was Conrad and I started to see each other. It started out as just a drink one Friday night and that turned into a couple of dates, nothing heavy and I really enjoyed his company. On the first occasion that he came to mine for dinner, Jasper sat on the arm of his chair and stared really hard at him. Conrad tried to move Jasper, but no sooner had he placed my cat on the mat, Jasper would leap back onto the arm of the chair again. Finally when Conrad resigned himself to just leaving the cat there, Jasper stepped onto Conrad's lap. He had somehow managed to find the best place to flex his claws, causing Conrad to suddenly hiss in pain. Jasper seemed not to notice and instead merely turned around twice and settled down to sleep, forcing Conrad to sit still. If Conrad even so much as shifted in his chair, Jasper let out a loud growl that was beyond threatening. It was as if the cat was acting as a chaperone and ensuring that Conrad kept his hands to himself. At exactly eleven o'clock that evening, Jasper awoke. Poor Conrad had been forced to eat his dinner without moving from the chair, which given that we had decided on a meal and a movie, worked out OK. The film finished at about half past ten and Jasper was fast asleep. At eleven, Jasper awoke, jumped from Conrad's lap and seemed to use his claws to pulled Conrad from the chair. Luckily for me, Conrad was a good man and had mentioned that he needed to head home anyway, but Jasper's insistence just seemed to make it more obvious that my cat was not yet ready to share me and my bed with another person.

It was another two months before Conrad was able to stay over and I was already back at school for the autumn term. Unfortunately as is so often the case in autumn, I caught the first flu of the year and was sent home from work shivering and almost crying. The head of my department herself drove me home and made me promise to go straight to bed. Once in bed, I phoned Conrad and he agreed to visit me as soon as he finished work that evening. He arrived at almost dead on six and Jasper was fretting over me as I lay in bed. As Conrad climbed the stairs to my room, Jasper mid head bump, turned his gaze towards the bedroom door and almost seemed to sigh thankfully. As Conrad came in, Jasper shot past him and dashed down the stairs. Conrad had not even had time to sit down before we heard the sound of the cat flap and Jasper disappearing outside.

Conrad had bought me a bunch of flowers, a box of lemsip and a bottle of apple juice, none of which I had asked for and all of which I very much appreciated. I don't know when it happened, but I fell asleep and when I awoke, Jasper was fast asleep on my pillow and next to him was a note written by Conrad. He had gone home to shower and change his clothes and he promised to return later and maybe even bring a curry. I flicked on the television and once again fell asleep with in minutes and dreamt of strange news events and cat purring. When I next woke up, Conrad was sat on the bed next to me, his bare feet poking out of the end of his jeans and he and Jasper were both tucking into a curry. I watched for a few minutes, amused to see my boys bonding so well until Jasper looked up and saw that I was awake. He pranced across the duvet and started rubbing his head against mine and then climbed across me and started rubbing his head against Conrad's side. Once he had made it clear that he approved of Conrad looking after me, he returned to his curry and then went to sleep on the end of the bed. I snuggled into Conrad's arms and slept through until morning.

I returned to work once my flu had gone enough that I could function and was quickly back into the swing of work. However, I had a lot of marking to catch up on and I also had to ensure that I was up to date with my continued professional development work. To do this work in the evenings, I needed to lay in bed with my laptop and log on to the school website. Yet strangely my home network seemed to fail. For three hours I struggled to log on, but it just refused to work, I could not even make Facebook work and there was no chance of skyping Conrad who was away in North Wales on a big hotel job with his crew. I reset the router, I turned it off and waited for ten seconds before turning it on again and in the end, I made a phone call to the company who provided my internet connection. They assured me that it was working fine and said that if it was not, I would likely need to change my router that took the signal from the phone line. I slammed the phone down furiously, after all, how could a device that had worked perfectly for months, suddenly stop working just when I needed it? It never occurred to me that other hands had been at work. I stalked into my office and once again angrily switched off the router, but it was only then that I noticed that something had changed. I stared at it intently, something was different, something was missing. I searched the floor, I checked my desk and turned over every paper and book sat there waiting for me, but there was no sign of the aerial for the wireless.

I turned the place almost upside down looking for it and finally at half past eleven that night, I gave up and decided that I would have to replace it the next day. It was only when I climbed into bed that I spotted Jasper, curled up asleep on the bed next to where I slept, his little arms clutching the very same aerial that I had been searching for so hard. I went to move it from his grasp and as I did so, he let out a low evil growl and opened a single eye to watch my hand retreat back to my side of the bed. As an experiment, I stroked his chin which resulted in loud purrs and then I scratched gently behind his ears and again I was treated to loud purrs, but as I moved my hand towards the piece of my router, the purr changed to low rumbling growl. Given that it was so late, I decided against doing any work anyway and being quite tired was soon asleep. When I awoke the next morning Jasper was gone from the bed and so was the aerial. I stumbled into my office and found it screwed back into the router and my Wi-Fi was working once again. Jasper was no where to be seen.

Conrad and I had been together for three years and had been living together for a year when he proposed to me. It was all very nice and in a way quite romantic. When he asked me, he gave me a beautiful ring and also presented Jasper with a new collar that was very smart. He put the ring on my finger and the new collar on Jasper and I knew then, that our family was pretty much set. The wedding was really nice, not a big affair and we decided to take Jasper with us, which meant putting him on a lead. When I tried, Jasper went ballistic and was thrashing and growling until I released him, much to Conrad's hilarity. I gave up on the lead and Jasper crept off to the end of the bed, his ears flat on his head, his eyes angry black holes. If I even so much as went near him, the cat equivalent of go away was growled at me. Conrad however simply picked Jasper up and carrying him baby like wandered off down stairs. I could hear Conrad explaining it to Jasper, as if he were a human child and weirdly, I could have sworn that I heard a small voice replying to him in English. Moments later Conrad climbed the stairs with Jasper, tail erect, full of purrs and walking on a lead. On the day of the wedding, Jasper carried the rings in a tiny box attached to his collar and the registrar stated that he had never before seen such a well trained and perfectly behaved cat. It was only then that

Jasper jumped into the plastic plants and wee'd on the artificial soil!

Conrad was away on another big contract and I had been promoted at work to head of department, which meant that I was working flat out. I was anxious, working almost every waking hour and with Conrad away, was not talking to anyone other than work until his brief phone calls in the evenings. I was, if I am honest, probably working towards a burn out and I was exhausted. The phone rang while I was in the bath and it was that sound that woke me up. I was just trying to stand up when the ringing stopped and then I heard the small voice once again. Whoever it was talking, knew Conrad well enough to joke with him on the phone. The voice was small, clearly male and English was fairly obviously a second language. I froze at the thought of a strange man in my home and did what was the only sensible thing. I wrapped myself in my towel and my dressing gown and charged into the bedroom.

The phone lay on the bed, I could hear Conrad's voice suddenly confused and I grabbed it up urgently to tell him about the strange man in my house. Jasper crept out from under the bed and jumped up onto the duvet. His eyes were sheepish and his purrs were just him repeating the word purr purr. He sat down and stared at me silently while I tried to work out what was going on. Finally I spoke to Conrad and asked him who he had been talking to. I was a bit shocked when he said Jasper. Jasper had been licking his front paws and suddenly stopped, looked up and spoke. "It's true you know, Conrad and I are from the same planet."

I dropped the phone in shock and stared in disbelief at Jasper. He jumped off the bed and wandered over to the phone and spoke into it, telling Conrad to call back in a few minutes. He then jumped back onto the bed and sat down, where he patted the bed indicating that I too should sit down. He explained to me how he and Conrad had travelled across deepest space to find a planet where they could settle down and be happy. They had not come together and it had been a chance encounter that had revealed their true origins to each other. I was silently hoping that the talking cat on my bed was the result of a breakdown due to overwork, but it clearly was not when my phone rang and Conrad confirmed what Jasper had told me.

So after so many years of Jasper and then Conrad living with me, I faced the truth of knowing that my husband and my pet were aliens. Jasper said that he was relieved that he had finally been able to tell me and Conrad was just the same as he was before, although he worked away less. Things have changed in our home now, Jasper has his own room and also has his own laptop. I dread to think what it is that he looks at on line, but I recently received a LOL-Cats tea towel in the mail because he had been using my bank card to pay for something on line.

I am still a teacher, some things never change, but I stepped down from head of department and went back to being an ordinary teacher. Life goes on and I get more time to spend with my boys. The great thing about modern travel is that Jasper has his own passport, which means he can travel almost anywhere in the world, as long as he is with Conrad and I. However, both him and Conrad have told me that when we are all ready to retire, we are not staying here, in this old house. Conrad wants to see the rest of the galaxy and I have never been out of Europe. I can only imagine what it is like out there among the stars.

Fly on the wall

By Sally Ann Nixon

What do I see? I see everything. I see you but you don't see me. I know where the spider lurks and the cat leaps. I know about the sticky strips that you hang up to trap me and I watch you spray poison to kill me. But you don't see me.

Summer is best. In winter, I can only hide in dark corners and dodge spiders but food is scarce. In summer food is everywhere. Your bin bags, rotting fruit and vegetables on the turn. Your compost heaps, fast food dumped on the pavement, left over barbecues . Anything old, anything rotten or left.

But what else do I see?

I see everything.

From your birth to your death I am there.
What I could tell you if I so wished.
Where your husband goes when he works late. Who your wife sees on her evenings out with the girls.
What your children do when you are not there.
Who smokes tobacco. Who smokes weed. Who snorts cocaine.
Who injects other things.
Who stalks in the night and commits small sins in the day.
The deeper and darker the secret, the more that I see.

My heart, if I had one, rejoices in the beat of of a techno rave with its sweat and vomit. The first cry of new life attracts me as does the vague fog of death. All hold promise for me.

You give me no respect. But my babes eat up your mess. They used to clean your wounds and infections from your ears. We can tell you who died when and where the bodies are buried. But you see us as wholly bad. Useless. Or else the friends of the vampire, the companions of Beelzebub. So does that make us a sorts of demon, dark Gods, potent powers in the land?

But when all is said and done, I'm only a fly. Something you swat and curse, buzzing and hoping and feeding and dying. Just like you.

And I see everything.

Lay-bys

By Geraldine Paige.

Pre-dawn. At a litter filled lay-by. Benedict Ironforge and Major Alice Redd would have their tryst. It is not the most romantic of places. But it is convenient. When Bendy Dick (Alice's nick name for him) had finished making love to her, he would throw his used condom out of the car window along with all the others. It is said that most people sleep heavier at pre-dawn. In this couples case. It is correct, which makes it perfect for them to tip-toe out without disturbing their other half's. Everything went swimmingly. Until. Horror of Horror's. The lay-by was cleaned up and turned into a lay-by garden. The couple were devastated. For week's they hunted around for another place. Until one night out of the blue, scarecrow's started to appear. Not just one, but couples. They would be in fields and garden's. Then in the morning, gone. As it turned out, the lay-by that Bendy Dick and Alice Redd used for their tryst, was also used by many other couples doing the same thing. So when they found out about the lay-by. They dressed themselves up as scarecrows, so that they could have sex in the field's and garden's and on one would be any the wiser.

Lady Killgallen

By Michael Low

The Silver Wraith pulled up slowly adjacent to the main entrance of The Ritz hotel. It was a warm September evening and all seemed so quiet and nice. The Ritz doorman opened the passenger door and held it whilst standing perfectly still. The long elegant legs that first showed themselves through the doorway were followed by the immaculately dressed figure of a bonneted lady robed and bejewelled in the most luxurious manner.

'Good evening, your Ladyship.' Said the doorman.

'Thank you.' Responded the Lady who then turned towards the driver and said 'Please collect me at 10.00, our meal will be over by then.'

'Yes Ma'am' came the respond from behind the wheel.

The Lady climbed the steps to the entrance door which was held open for her by the other doorman, and upon entering she was meet by the smiling faces of a well-dressed couple of men, who had obviously been waiting for her arrival and they both greeted her with enthusiasm.

'So glad you could make it my Lady. Let me introduce Thomas Mulready to you he is the Chief Executive Officer of the Almac mining company.'

'So pleased to meet you Lady Killgallen. It's a pleasure.' Said Thomas Mulready as he nodded towards her and held out his hand, which was accepted by Lady Killgallen.

'Please you may call me Carol.' Said the Lady.

'Our table is ready, my Lady. Please follow me.' And with that comment, James Doncaster, who was Lady Killgallen's employee, turned and led them towards the Ritz dining room at the end of the corridor. The piano situated halfway down the corridor was being played as they passed. Lady Killgallen stopped momentarily at the piano and looking at the pianist who was facing her said:

'Please play some of Frank Sinatra's music, you know it's my favourite.'

'Certainly my Lady.' Said the pianist with a smile, he was obviously very familiar with her and her taste in music for he quickly finished what he was playing and then continued with 'My Way' one of Sinatra's big hits.

James led them to a table in the corner of the restaurant near to a window. It was immaculately laid out for dinner and they could hear the pianist playing when they sat down.

The three of them picked up their menu's and proceeded to deliberate on what they would eat this evening.

'May I get you some drinks?' The waiter stood slightly leaning forward as he addressed the group.

'Bucks Fizz for me' said Lady Killgallen.

'I'll have a glass of merlot please' said Thomas

'Me too' said James. 'I'll order a bottle, we can share it then.

'Great!' Was the response from Thomas, who was finding it quite difficult to keep his eyes off of Lady Killgallen. He thought she looked gorgeous. Her eyes were a light mesmerising blue and her outfit seemed to gleam in the light as it enhanced her almost hour glass figure. The diamond brooch on her tunic and the similar diamond earrings she wore all added to the overwhelming effect she had on him. What a woman! He thought. It was a pity that he had come here on business to discuss things with the owner of the land his company wanted to buy. Given other circumstances, he felt sure he would probably try to make a date with her.

The waiter retuned to the table with their drinks and then took their food orders.

'Thank you for coming to meet me Carol.' Said Thomas raising his glass of Merlot towards her, the three of them toasted together.

'Now, let's get down to business. Said Carol.

'Well, it's like this.' Said Thomas looking serious, 'the parcel of land my company wants from you is just the five acres adjoining our factory in Kent. I feel sure that the land is not of much use to you, my Lady, but it would be very useful to us, you see it would enable us to extend our facilities allowing us to grow and expand our business. I'm sure we can meet the price you might be considering for it.'

'Not so fast Mr Mulready. That land also adjoins my estate and I would not want the view from my bedroom window to be marred by a collection of factories and offices that you might build there.'

'But it's half a mile further down to your house, surely whatever we build there would hardly have much impact on your outlook.'

'Yes it would, of course it would. My family have lived in Hockney Hall for over 200 years, and have enjoyed it there. I think your plans would ruin everything.'

'Oh please my Lady, surely we can reach some arrangement. I have been given the authority by the board to make you a very good offer. How much would you want for the five acres?'

'They are not for sale, unless you can guarantee not to build anything on them without my permission.'

James Doncaster sat, listening to the conversation between my Lady and Mulready, just playing with his meal which had been delivered by the waiter while they were talking. He was not surprised at all by Lady Killgallen's stance concerning the sale of the land. He knew she certainly did not need the money, and the thought of changing the area surrounding Hockney Hall was not to be contemplated.

Thomas Mulready was looking down at his baked salmon and greens, he suddenly looked up and said:

'OK. Would £5,000,000 be enough?'

Lady Killgallen did not hesitate for a second.

'No. Unless you give me the required guarantees regarding any building work.'

'I cannot do that. However there is one other thing I could do to help.'

'What is that?'

'I could keep secret the details of your affair with Lord Snaith of Castle Cameron, which has been going on for over a year, and would, if it became public, have serious impact on his marriage and on your reputation. You choose!'

My Lady had dropped her fork on the plate and stared at Mulready in disbelief.

'You are not serious. It's not true.'

'Oh yes it is, I have the photographs to prove it and we have been monitoring the relationship for some time through our private detective agency where they have recorded times and places of your nefarious meetings. Don't tell me it's not true!'

Lady Killgallen had stopped eating. The whole atmosphere at the table had changed into one of adversity and malice. James Doncaster looked across at Mulready and said:

'I think we should terminate this meeting now. This is neither the time nor place to discuss these things.'

Have it your way then, but if I do not get an agreement today then we will make sure that the details of the affair are published. Your reputation will be in tatters, Lady Killgallen!'

My Lady pushed her unfinished meal away from her and stood

142

up turning to Doncaster she said:

'Please ring my driver now and just walk me to the entrance. I will leave you with Mr Mulready to finish your meal.'

Doncaster did as he was told and walked with my Lady to the Ritz doorway.

'What shall I do my Lady?' He said as they reached the exit.

'You must finish your meal with him then take him back to his hotel. Make sure that you are seen leaving him alone, then return disguised and kill him. Do you understand?'

'Yes My Lady.'

'That will be all, Doncaster.'

Magpies

By Jayne Hecate

"Barry mate, I'm not sure that it is that simple. I suppose if you applied the grease to them directly, I reckon you could probably do it." Dex sighed, "but why would you want to?"

Barry looked doubtful. "I am telling you Dex, they are too big, birds like that just wont fit, you need smaller ones mate. I suppose that you could use a couple of finches, maybe even a budgie, although they tend to bite because they are vicious little bastards."

"The thing is Barry, going bigger, would give a stronger reaction. Imagine how it would feel with one of them?" Both men watched the magpies as they cursed and chittered at each other. "One of them would be a struggle to get in, but once in, well can you imagine?"

"I can imagine the face of the medic who has to pull it out and an angry magpie is not going to come out easily. Also, that beak is going to do some damage Dex." Barry continued to frown.

"You could always tape the beak up, a bit of electrical tape would work well enough." Dex countered.

"Why is it always electrical tape with you mate?" Barry did not look happy and shook his head in frustration. "In fact why do we always end up having this conversation? Why can't you just say oh look at that Barry, what a lovely magpie? But oh no not you, not our Dex. It is always the same with you, oh look at that lovely magpie, can you imagine how that feel if you stuck it up your arse?" Dex grinned red faced, Barry continued. "There is something wrong with you mate, you need help."

"Yeah, you are right Barry... I could never catch them on my own!"

Haunted Ice

By Geraldine Paige

The local Ice Rink is famous for the amount of Champion Ice Skaters it has produced . When I say Skater`s , I mean, the whole range of skating activities. Mothers have been known to put their children`s names down before they could walk, just to make sure of a place. 'J' (real name Joy) and her husband Edward, are the Rink owners.

The only thing that really matters to `J` and Edward, is winning Competitions, they can not resist it, it`s like a drug. One Autumn morning `J` received an invitation for a competition to be held at Tern Manor. The participants must be between 18 and 21 years of age. The event will be on Christmas Eve, everyone would have to spend Christmas Day and Boxing Day at the Manor. The Competition will consist of one female and one male figure skater and one dance couple. `J` and her team will be competing against the local neighbouring Ice Rink Club. Each Club is allowed one person over the age of 25 to help keep an eye on things. The number of bedrooms are limited, so parents are not invited. Hooray thought `J`. no interference from Mum and Dad, I will have a free hand. I`ll make them work.

The night before `J` and her skaters left for Tern Manor, `J` made a space on her trophy shelf, stood back, had a good long look. Yes. She thought. Three trophies will look good there. Then she boarded the mini bus.

Tern Manor was a beautiful large family home situated by the sea, every year Terns would nest there. Hence the name Tern Manor. The family that built it still lived there, and are able to trace their history back to Henry V111. The ice rink is an extension of the Manor, and one could see that no expense was spared when it was built.

Christmas Eve. `J`s male figure skater won. `J`s female figure skater was not so lucky. One trophy gone, the dancers had better not let me down thought `J`. The Lord and Lady of the Manor just smiled to themselves when they saw that `J` was getting angry with her team.

Did `J` go home with one or two trophies? In fact. No one went home at all.

It all started the day `J` had picked their daughter to compete in a figure skating competition. They built the ice rink for her to practice in. And she did, almost non stop. She won. But paid a heavy price. She had worked so hard to please `J` that her health broke, she never recovered and past away. The parents blamed `J` for overworking her. `J` did not care, she had her trophy.

Their daughter`s ghost haunts the ice rink day and night. She is unable to rest in peace until justice has been done. Her parent`s knew that `J` could not resist a competition. You can see them now skating around and around, until, one by one they drop. It`s true. Revenge is best served cold. And what`s colder than an Ice Rink.?.

Maggie's Dedication

by Sally Ann Nixon

An odd little town this. Set in a time warp. The police put out a notice for a public meeting about future policy. Resolved on face book. The lady who ran the Post Office closed it and converted it to a dress and fancy goods shop. So we only have a post office van in the Square once a week and that tends to break down and go home. We've been promised a proper post office in September but no one holds their breath. Sheep racing in October, Celtic Music in August. A certain Ealing comedy eccentricity at all times Inconvenient but the place has charm. 'Quirky', is probably the right word for it.

Take a small incident only last week. We've a number of charity shops in town. Red Cross, Animal Welfare but the best is ' The Cat House', which supports stray cats, neuters feral cats and has the best selection of unwanted gifts, bric a brac and second hand clothes for miles. Eluned spotted them and the word went out....

"'Cat House' has surplus stock thermal undies. In their bags. Cheap!"

Now this is a cold, wet part of the world. Thermal undies are not a fashion statement - they are a survival necessity. They came in sizes up to XXL too, which is great because we can get two layers of them under our woolies and fleeces. But we had to hurry or they would be sold out.
"And in the meantime try to keep it quiet", said Eluned or there would be a run on them.

We gathered in Tudor's Cafe and set forth with battle in our eyes and greed in our hearts. Those thermals were OURS!
But 'The Cat House' was shut. Lights off, door locked, only a selection of bedding pansies outside, next to the honesty box.
A paper bag with a message was sellotaped to the inside of the door.

Shop Closed.

Locked inside with dog.

LOO BLOCKED.

Awaiting plumber.

So that was that. Maggie had locked herself somewhere inside with her Yorkie and we wasn't coming out till the plumber came. We could see the cardboard box marked thermals through the window. Eluned sent a text.
"Maggie. Its us. Do you need a sandwich? Keep some thermals back for us."
A tremulous reply came back.
" Myself and Mr Bones are staying until help arrives. We are at the back and we have have our salad sandwiches and tea. We will keep some thermals back for you. We will not desert our post".
No arguing with that. We went for another cuppa, toasted Maggie's dedication and lived to fight another day.

Monster

By Jayne Hecate

"Rodney Graham Hoskins!" The voice was shrill and clearly belonged to an elderly and very well spoken lady, of a certain class and sophistication. "Monster has done his business in the hallways, come and clean it up at once!"

"Yes Mum!" he called back down the stairs jovially, "I will be right there!"

Rodney pulled on his large black ex military boots, the sole of the left boot was worn so thin that that the rubber had started to give way to the thin hardboard base, but it was in better condition than the right, upon which the front of the boot had parted company with the sole and it flapped as he walked, giving him the sound of a flip flop wearer, which when the streets were covered in snow seemed to amuse more than inconvenience him.

"Oh Rodney, he is weeing on the mat by the kitchen floor now, when are you going to walk the poor animal?"

Rodney pulled on his thick heavily stained leather biker jacket, the front had seen more than fifteen summers of riding since he had bought it second hand from the covered market. The silver pen and spray painted names of bands had faded into the grey of the leather, which had in turn faded at the edges into a dirty white. "I'm coming Mum!" He slid through the door of his room and descended the stairs rapidly, reaching into his pocket for a poo bag and the lead he used when walking Monster.

Monster stood in the kitchen doorway, his teeth bared into a vicious looking snarl, but his back knees seemed to be trembling and Rodney gently scratched him affectionately between the ears and clipped on the lead. He scraped up the small hard droppings into the plastic bag and dropped it into the kitchen bin and then stepped through the backdoor to the garden, Monster following faithfully on his lead. For a moment Rodney paused and then he leaned back in through the door. "Back in half an hour Mum, just taking Monster for his walk." If she replied, he did not hear as he pulled the door closed behind him.

Monster jumped along the path to the garden gate, he moved so smoothly, he barely looked disabled at all, but with a missing front leg, his walks tended to take a bit of time, especially as he seemed to enjoy sniffing through the hedges and along the canal tow path.

Rodney was tall, technically he was six foot, six and half inches tall, but the green mohican put him at close to seven feet. He was also heavily tattooed down both arms and one or two of them even stretched onto his hands. However, the tattoos did not extend above his collarbones, at his Mother's firm insistence. His eyes were pale blue, almost a greeny grey and even when out of focus due to what ever drink or drug he could put down his throat, they always managed to sparkle in a way that made him look friendly. The elderly ladies that made up his Mother's circle of friends always gave him a peck on the cheek, if he was home when they visited, treating him as some sort of slightly wayward, but deeply beloved nephew. If he was away from home, they would ask after him and it was always with a small amount of pride that his Mother would explain that her only child, a slender young man of forty three, unmarried, childless and probably eternally single, was out fighting fox hunting or protesting some industrial site that was fracking a natural beauty spot, often accompanied by his faithful Monster.

During the protests when developers had wanted to build a large shed on a patch of ancient woodland just outside the village, the local Police had eyed Rodney with a sense of trepidation and maybe a little worry because he looked like a fearsome creature and his unusual pet was equally aggressive looking. Yet when they finally arrested him for sitting in the road, blocking the way of a large truck carrying concrete, he had resisted gently and politely as he and Monster were lifted with some difficulty into the back of a Police van. When he arrived at the cells, the arresting officer had actually been to school with and quite liked Rodney, making sure that he was given as much comfort as possible, even though he was technically a law breaker. As for Monster, when Rodney handed over the paperwork that showed that he was legitimately kept, he was placed into the old dog pen at the back of the station and the younger officers stared at him with some fascination.

Monster had quickly been released when a stern and forthright elderly woman dressed in a smart woollen suite and pearls had arrived at the station, demanding to know where both her son and her pet badger were. The Police were more than happy to release Monster into her care, but Rodney had been forced to wait a further three hours before he too was released into the care of his Mother before the charges were finally dropped.

Monster had come into Rodney's life in a dramatic way, having been a rescue. It was thought that he had been hit by a fleeing car after hunt sabs had witnessed the local hunt trespassing on private land owned by a local conservation charity. The Police had been called, but with the chief inspector being a member of the hunt too, the young officers did very little to intervene. The car was driven by one of the hunt supporters and had hit monster which had bounced him into the hedgerow, where he lay unseen for around three hours before Rodney found him, close to death. Despite the blood, Rodney had scooped the animal up and with no other way of carrying him, tucked him into his bike jacket and did it up as best as he could. The ride to the village vets had been fraught with worry, if the animal had struggled, it was entirely possible that Rodney could suddenly face having a wild and angered badger fighting to be free of his jacket, as he rode his old Honda sportsbike along a little more sedately than usual. Strangely Monster had seemed to trust Rodney from the start and instead of struggling, had just lay against Rodney's chest, gently panting and occasionally licking at a wound. The first vet to examine Monster declared him un-savable and it was only Rodney's powerful insistence that another vet be brought into the room to examine the injured badger more thoroughly. Monster was very badly hurt and his front leg was horrifically broken and had been almost completely torn off. The vet did her best, but said with some sadness that it was unlikely that he would survive. Rodney said that he wanted the very best care for his badger and said that he would pay whatever it cost to make him better. He listened carefully as the vet explained that the animal would probably need to go to a specialist home, a place where disabled wild life could live out their lives in safety and comfort. Rodney shook his head and stated firmly that the animal was coming home with him and as if to confirm this, the animal had, despite its terrible injuries, climbed into his arms and gently began to lick his hand.

The first walks with Monster had been interesting, he was terrified of cars, which was unsurprising, but with gentle perseverance and a lot of treats, he slowly started accepting his new more metropolitan life. It took months for him to relax at the sound of a dog though and Rodney had more than once had to reassure a worried looking dog owner who expressed concern that a huge punk rocker was being savaged by a large angry looking badger!

Rodney and Monster had later moved in with Rodney's Mum after Rodney found that vet bills made paying the rent on his small flat rather hard. His Mum had lived alone and since the death of her husband was a little lonely, so having her only son move back home was in some ways a blessing for her, but it had taken some time for her and Monster to get used to each other. Rodney knew that they had finally bonded when he came home late from a gig in London and found the badger fast sleep on the sofa, snuggled into close to the elderly woman, who was also gently snoring, her hand resting lovingly on the course fur of the badger. Rodney had grinned at them both and then he carefully tucked her blanket around her and slid her slippers from her feet as he settled down in his Dad's old chair to read his book and wait for the effects of his last dab of speed to wear off. Monster opened one eye for a brief moment and after a small snort and a gentle whiffle, seemed to settle back even deeper into the old lady's legs.

The walk lasted the usual half and hour and Rodney noticed that

Monster seemed to tire a little more quickly than usual. When he had rescued Monster, he had not been sure how old he was and the vet was not entirely sure either, but after five years, Monster was starting to look a little grey around the black parts of his fur. With winter approaching, his old joints were probably getting stiff and maybe even a little arthritic. Back at the garden, Rodney released Monster from his lead and the badger had a little sniff around in the garden before heading to the backdoor which he pushed open with his snout and disappeared inside. Rodney stamped his boots free of the mud from the tow path and wandered inside.

Monster was snuffling on the sofa with Rodney's Mum and she had an open packet of dog treats in her hand, gently feeding him the little snacks. She looked up and smiled at her son as he grinned at her from the doorway. "You want a cuppa Mum?"

"Yes please my darling, why don't you fill the pot and then we can listen to that new demo you told me about?"

Rodney laughed, it amused him greatly that his eighty year old Mother, a woman of high standing in the local community and proficient knitter of pink cardies for various local babies, enjoyed the obscure New York hardcore punk that he loved so much. Rodney filled the kettle from the warm kitchen tap and put it on the stove to boil. He turned and leaned against the kitchen side and looked through the open door to where Monster was settling down in his little bed, next to his Mother's own comfortable place on the sofa. It was a brief moment of serenity in an otherwise chaotic universe and for a tiny dark moment, Rodney wondered how long it could last?

Graduation Day

By Margaret Ingram

I'm walking down the aisle of Bristol Cathedral and remembering another procession 62 years ago.

My gown floats around me today but then it was heavier material and I held the front up slightly as I walked. The old pink curtains that had been cut up to make that gown were decorated with pearl beads and the standing collar behind my head was edged with tiny pearls, too. The hood of my gown today is the same pink as the curtains were.

That day was my mother's fortieth birthday, though I don't remember anyone mentioning it then. It's only recently I've even worked that one out and it might explain why Mum was in such a foul mood. It was one of the few times I remember her getting drunk. Everyone was celebrating a different woman getting crowned that 2nd of June.

We had a TV with an enormous 10 inch screen and the whole family were watching the coronation on it in our front room. I was dressed and taken round to the fancy dress contest by my sister, who left me there and rushed back to watch the box again. All the kids in fancy dress were marshalled into a procession and we marched around the hall. I was five, almost six and probably the only child there on their own, everyone else's family were clapping and cheering them on. I didn't mind, anyway, since the clapping overlapped and some of the adults were saying nice things about the Elizabethan dress I presented. It was the best costume by far, and each elimination round thinned out my competition. The final choice saw me win, at which point I started to learn a salutary lesson in life. The mother of the second prize winner, whose costume of crepe paper in red, white and blue could just as well have won a French parade, started arguing. After a fraught 5 minutes the judges capitulated and I got the second prize while she got first.

To be honest, I didn't really care. I felt I had been chosen and the final result was typical of my life, where younger cousins or older people's needs always seemed to come before mine. I liked my dress, I was pleased that everyone had seen me win. I went home and showed the family my second prize, a cast-iron moneybox in the shape of a crown. It never worked properly and I never saved money, but it was a Prize!

Today was similar, but this time I had been acknowledged, my graduation was undeniable and I felt I was the only person there who fully understood the wonderful feeling of winning the parade. 62 years have taught me that I am the only one who can make me feel this good and I don't need to be given the prize when I can take it for myself.

WINTER

By Geraldine Paige

Stand Aside Winter has arrived.
She covers the land with her thick white blanket.
A job that only Winter can do.
Yes. She can be harsh like a Mother making her offspring do
something that must be done.
The land must live.
We must live.
The land must rest.
We must rest.
We must feed.
The land must feed.
That's why Winter has arrived.
So. Stand aside, Winter has arrived.

The Barbeque

By Nim Mangat

Angela watched her friends from the kitchen window, as they settled themselves down around the barbeque – well, she used the word 'friends' loosely, more like her colleagues. People who had treated her like a skivvy, 'run and photocopy this, dear', 'do get me a latte and a sandwich from Pret, dear' or 'here's fifty quid, get something suitable for my eleven year old daughter and get it wrapped and send it round to my house, dear'. Yet, she wasn't sure if, after three years, any of them even knew her name.

She invited them into her home the weekend before she was to leave the office, to go travelling around the world on her own.

She knew all eight of them would accept her invitation out of morbid curiosity, knew they had been discussing it at length.

Fortunately, the weather was fine. The barbeque lit, the steaks and ribs marinating in the fridge, the selection of salads already on the small, folding table beside them.

They had arrived in a steady stream as if they had all planned to be there at the same time. She took their jackets and showed them into her small, but tastefully decorated monochrome lounge, where they ooohed in surprise. They eyed up her selection of beautifully crafted artefacts and black and white photographs. John from Finance said, 'I didn't know you had a Great Dane – I have one too!'

She ushered them out through the French windows, to the sunny patio, filled with perfumed geraniums. They made themselves comfortable on the white, cast iron chairs and accepted the handmade canapés and pink prosecco that she offered. Soon their mindless chatter filled the garden as Angela expertly threw marinated steaks, ribs and kebabs, threaded onto long metal skewers, on to the hot barbeque and watched them sizzle and send up puffs of white smoke. She offered them around with salads and dips and sourdough bread. They commented how they were cooked to perfection and devoured the food hungrily.

'Aren't you having any,' they asked.

'I'm vegetarian,' Angela replied, as she passed around the last of the ribs.

'Oh, I didn't know that?' said Clare from Data.

Later, when the conversation had dried up and there was a certain amount of discomfort among the guests, they mumbled about forgotten meetings, visits from family, or throbbing headaches. They made their apologies and thanked her for a lovely afternoon.

'Enjoy your travels!' they said, 'Don't forget to send us a postcard!'

'Your Great Dane,' asked John from finance, just as he was leaving, 'what was his name?'

'Chancer.'

'Interesting name – looks very handsome.'

She closed the door on her last guest.

Yes, Chancer was a very handsome fellow, good enough to eat. Angela hummed a vaguely remembered tune, as she skipped through the French windows to the back garden, with a black bin liner.

Writing for Posterity

By Mike Low

I remember, some time ago now, when I was asked what it was that I considered the most attractive asset a lady could possess. The expected answer of facial beauty, body dimensions, sexual proclivity etc. was not given by me. I responded with the answer 'a sense of humour'. Which was received initially in silence by the questioner and the small group of ladies who were listening. There then followed a small amount of muttering and what I can only describe as a degree of disbelief amongst my listeners, the conversation then moved on to another subject.

I will say that without a sense of humour life could be unbearable. One has to have a sense of humour if one wants to enjoy life and be a good friend to others. There are a couple of examples that stick in my mind and please let me share them with you.

When I was 16 years old in 1964, I began my engineering apprenticeship with the then Bristol Siddeley Engine Corporation in Bristol in the company of about 20-odd others of similar age. We were all looking forward to a five-year apprenticeship culminating in our status as an engineer earning a not inconsiderable wage. After about 6 months our group was sent to a classroom where we were to be given a lecture by, we were told, an officer from the RAF. Bearing in mind that this period was during the Cold War and we were involved in manufacturing aero engines for our fighters and bombers, I think we could all understand the relevance of being given a talk by someone who appreciated the importance of what we were involved in doing.

The officer was introduced to us all and, judging by his age, most of us assumed that he had seen service in WWII. We sat silently while he began talking to us and he opened the lecture by saying:-

'Now I know that most of you will think that all we pilots in the RAF are a bunch of heroic, devil- may- care, beer-swilling layabouts. Well I'm here to refute that pack of lies. I can assure you all that we are just beer-swilling layabouts!'

The one second silence that followed was broken by spontaneous laughter from us all. I learnt an important lesson from the RAF officers' talk that I've taken through my life – a sense of humour is very important. No, it's the most important asset any personality can possess.

A further example came from another RAF officer some 50 odd years later. My book on the Merlin aero engine 'The Saviour of the Free World' had just been published and I was fortunate enough to meet George 'Johnny' Johnson, born in 1921, who is the last surviving member of the RAF Dam Busters squadron. We met in the restaurant in the care home in Bristol where Johnny lives. Johnny was very nice to meet and we had an interesting conversation over a nice meal talking about the Merlin engine and other related topics. When the waiter seated us at our table I was a little nervous and decided to open the conversation by offering to pour Johnny some of the water on the table into his glass. I held the jug of water as I asked Johnny would he like some. He looked straight at me for a second and then said:-

'Water is for washing your hands. We'll have some red.'

Johnny was in his mid-nineties when we met at that time. I did just manage to keep up with him with the red wine. And, of course, Johnny confirmed again for me, the importance in life of a sense of humour.

About the Authors

Margaret Ingram is the vicious dictator of writing club, who makes us actually work and not just gossip. She lives in Somerset, but wishes it was in a volcano on a tropical island lair!

Sally Anne is a writer and inheritor of fine antiques, rescue cats, dogs, teenage boys and family furniture all of which need a lot of upkeep. Beloved among the group, she leads an eventful life, full of incidents that anyone sane would avoid. It does make good writing inspiration though!

Jan is a peaceful and ethereal young woman, with her heart and soul firmly placed in the land of fairy. A determined keeper of cats and ferrets, she can often be found in hedgerows fighting off little folk!

Geraldine likes to write short stories and poems. She also enjoys Spanish dancing and singing with her local choir. She is devilishly good fun with a subtly naughty side to her.

168

Nikki Pebble is a songwriter and performer, who was recently bullied into writing fiction, a field in which Nikki has excelled. When not writing, Nikki can found floating adrift at sea.

Mike Low is obsessed with football, putting his team above all things, even writing. Before he became a writer, Mike made the engines for death machines, which were sold to the Government. Mike has taught the more innocent members of the club about the intricacies of lay by usage and worries when we write stories about mariticide. Mike is married and lives in Somerset.

Nim Mangat is a fabulous, quirky and talented local writer. Handy with a quill pen, she can turn her mind to all types of prose, be it short stories, poems or threatening letters to the local paper.

Stephen Breakspear is a quantity Surveyor, who often surveys the quantities of puerile filth produced at writers club. He writes often funny, usually clever short stories that keep you holding on until the last word for the joke.

Jayne is a bleak, simple & misanthropic creature with a need to tell dark and evil stories. When not writing, she enjoys model making, listening to nihilistic and suicidal Black Metal or chasing villagers across the moors.

Carol is a Photographer, biker and the put upon Spouse of Jayne Hecate. When not snapping pics of her Motorbike, Carol can be found whizzing along the major roads of Britain, marveling at the beauty of the landscape or just trying to find a loo! She is also the photographer who provides our wonderful cover images.

Thanks

Thanks must go as always, to our Glorious Leader, the magnificent Head Honcho AKA Margaret, who writes all of our lessons, books the hall that we use, deals with all of the finances and supplies us with enthusiasm to continue with writing club, when she hasn't lost the village hall key. She is also the only one in the world who can talk Jayne into compiling these books for us!

We would also like to thank Carol for providing the cover photographs yet again. She very kindly supplied us with a selection of pictures for our first, second and now third book, from her collection.

Finally thank you to Jayne who compiled the book, worked out the formatting and transferred the files from the various types used by the group (without too much swearing, cursing or use of black magic), into yet another book.

RIP – Jayne's computer, which burned out a motherboard and destroyed several hard drives resulting in the loss of the first version of this completed book! Thank the maker for data back ups!

Printed in Great Britain
by Amazon